Praise for *The Gu..*

'Extraordinary: a unique blend of thriller, post-Covid dystopia and paean to the healing properties of nature'   *Guardian*

'Exceptionally good . . . A frighteningly plausible nightmare'
                                    Observer, Thriller of the Month

'Peter Heller's thrillers unfurl like campfire yarns'
                                                    New York Times

'Moves inexorably from natural elegy to a fast-paced and page-turning what-the-hell-is-going-on? Shades of nativist anti-cosmopolitanism, but first-rate'   *The Critic*

'An ever so subtly dystopian wilderness noir that speculates on the horrors of a post-pandemic society'   *USA Today*

'Riveting . . . A chilling reminder of the dangers that might lie in wait for us all'   *Minneapolis Star Tribune*

'A modern master of the wilderness thriller'   *Crime Reads*

'*The Guide* is a glorious getaway in every sense, a wild wilderness trip as well as a suspenseful journey to solve a chilling mystery'   *BookPage*

'Peter Heller is the poet laureate of the literary thriller, and *The Guide* offers further proof for the case. Powered by Heller's trademark prose, which alternately thunders and eddies like his beloved western rivers, this sinister and soulful story unfurls so skillfully that it's easy to ignore all the layers beneath – but you shouldn't. Heller writes about the eternal questions and the exquisite details, and he knows the places where they intersect in the human heart and the natural world'
                    Michael Koryta, *New York Times* bestselling author of
                                            Those Who Wish Me Dead

PETER HELLER is the award-winning author of *The Dog Stars*, a *New York Times* bestseller and a *Guardian*, *San Francisco Chronicle* and *Atlantic* Book of the Year, and *The River*, an *Observer* Thriller of the Year. Born and raised in New York, he has travelled the world as an expedition kayaker, writing about challenging descents in the Pamirs, the Tien Shan mountains, the Caucuses, Central America and Peru. He is a graduate of the Iowa Writers' Workshop, where he received an MFA in fiction and poetry, and won a Michener fellowship for his epic poem 'The Psalms of Malvine'.

ALSO BY PETER HELLER

FICTION

The River

Celine

The Painter

The Dog Stars

NONFICTION

Kook: What Surfing Taught Me About Love, Life, and Catching the Perfect Wave

The Whale Warriors: The Battle at the Bottom of the World to Save the Planet's Largest Mammals

Hell or High Water: Surviving Tibet's Tsangpo River

The Guide

PETER HELLER

WEIDENFELD & NICOLSON

First published in the United States in 2021 by Alfred A. Knopf,
a division of Penguin Random House LLC, New York

First published in Great Britain in 2021 by Weidenfeld & Nicolson,
This paperback edition first published in Great Britain
in 2022 by Weidenfeld & Nicolson,
an imprint of The Orion Publishing Group Ltd
Carmelite House, 50 Victoria Embankment
London EC4Y ODZ

An Hachette UK Company

1 3 5 7 9 10 8 6 4 2

A CIP catalogue record for this book is
available from the British Library.

ISBN (Mass Market Paperback) 978 1 4746 2390 2
ISBN (eBook) 978 1 4746 2391 9
ISBN (Audio) 978 1 4746 2392 6

Typeset by Born Group
Printed and bound in Great Britain by Clays Ltd, Elcograf S.p.A.

www.weidenfeldandnicolson.co.uk
www.orionbooks.co.uk

To Pop,
who made me laugh.
And who always took the longest view.

Kingfisher Lodge

1. MAIN LODGE
2. POOL HOUSE
3. MASSAGE CABIN
4,5,6. LARGE FAMILY CABINS
7. ALISON'S CABIN
8. JACK'S CABIN
9,10. SMALL CABINS
11. OFFICE AND FLY SHOP
12. ENTRY GATE
13. EQUIPMENT BARN

DON'T GET SHOT!

The Guide

They gave him a bunk in a cabin by the river. A wooded canyon, spruce and pine, with rimrock up high, and rock spurs that tumbled to the water.

Jack dropped his pack on the porch. It was a cool afternoon with high running clouds that tugged their shadows over the canyon. He looked around. The cabin was on the edge of a steep bank in the shadow of the pines, and a staggered rush rose from the creek below and was carried by the sift of wind in the trees. A creek, really. They called it a river, but up this high it was his favorite kind of stream: an easy toss of a stone across and shallow enough in places to wade bank to bank.

He studied the rhythm of it. It slid around a left bend and broke white through a jumble of boulders and coursed into a long black pool stuttered with smooth rocks. At the top of the pool he could see a pedestrian bridge, and a fishermen's trail heading upstream on the other side. Trout water out of a dream.

The shack was basic. On the narrow covered porch were a stack of split firewood and two cane rockers. He didn't really care what was inside: he thought he could sit on this deck and watch that stream for the rest of his life.

•

The lodge was booked solid from August twentieth, what the manager told him. They would close on October thirty-first or when the snow got too heavy, whichever came first. Jack would guide one fisher per day, or a couple, no more. Boutique fishing at its finest. Two hundred dollars a day plus tips, one day off every ten unless he wanted to skip it. Good money. Less than he could make running a drift boat on the Colorado, but it included food, lodging, and . . .

"Two drinks or two beers a night. After that, Ginnie cuts you off. We encourage the guides to hang out at the bar before dinner and converse with guests, but there's nothing sadder than a sodden fishing guide, am I right?"

That was the manager, Kurt Jensen, stepping onto the porch and handing him a card with the key code to open the heavy art gate at the head of the drive—two giant rusted cams that rocked apart with a grinding of heavy chains and cogs that slid thick steel doors etched with leaping trout.

"You'll need it to get out, and in."

"Why do you need a code to open it from the inside?" Jack said.

Kurt had pulled the screen and was shoving the cabin door with his shoulder. He was a big man, maybe six-one, wearing a cowboy hat and a wool vest. He was gray at the temples and had grainy blue eyes and Jack figured he was pushing fifty. "Door's sticky," Kurt said. "I can get you a palm sander tomorrow."

"Forget it, I've got a flat file in the truck, should work."

If Kurt heard him he didn't say. He was already inside, taking in the sparse log room: two small windows with tied-back lace curtains, a counter in back with a sink and two gas burners, a tiny bathroom with a shower stall, and an on-demand propane water heater on the wall. Baseboard electric heat and woodstove in the corner for ambiance, Jack guessed. For light two sconces—bare bulbs behind metal cutouts of bears, and a reading lamp on a barnwood bed table. A Nest thermostat on the wall by the door over the one small bureau. Quaint. The bed was full-size, just larger than a twin, with two Pendleton blankets. Perfect.

The cabin was pretty close quarters. Jack had a cloth face mask in his back pocket and he looped it over his ears and Kurt waved it away.

"You won't need that around here. It makes the guests uneasy. Fact is, everyone but you has been tested and Ginnie takes everyone's temperature when they come into the bar every night. You don't strike me as a hang-out-in-a-crowd type of guy, so I'm willing to take the risk."

"You were saying about the gate," Jack said.

"I was?"

"Yeah, why you need a code to open it. I mean from the inside."

"So nothing just hits the button, like a coyote or some blow-down. The last one we had was always opening on its own and all kinda random public was coming in and they'd just start fishing. Walk right past all the houses and fish, until we ran 'em off. God."

"Sounds rough," Jack said drily. If there was any sarcasm in Jack's tone it didn't register with the manager.

Kurt finished his survey and blew out with a near whistle. "You won't believe how crazy fishermen get around this river. The locals call our stretch Billionaire's Mile. It's the private water all mixed in with public. Us, the Taylor River Lodge downstream, a couple other outfits. I wish they'd just shut down the whole canyon, give the landowners some peace. You need matches for the woodstove, and an axe to split kindling."

"Got 'em," Jack said. He didn't mention that his own ranch on the Colorado—his and Pop's—was sandwiched between public water and they rarely had a problem.

"Okay, good. I'll help you with your stuff. Dinner's at six thirty. If you come early you can meet Cody, the other guide. And your client tomorrow. Her name is Alison K."

"K?"

"Famous. The famous guests use a lot of initials. Ha."

"Got it." Jack followed his boss out through the door and they walked up the short path to the pullout and Jack's truck.

"What's with the bike?" Jack said. There was a teal one-speed cruiser bicycle with a bell and basket. It stood on a kickstand in a patch of sunlight.

"Oh that, yeah. One per guest. See how everything's spread out?"

Kurt waved his arm up the hill to the scattering of cabins in the pines; then he nodded down the sanded dirt road to where Jack could just see the exquisite rambling log ranch house of the lodge and the small trout pond beside it. Hand-stacked stone chimneys, shallow rooflines with wide eaves and covered porches most of the way around. Rocking chairs and hanging geraniums. Jack nodded.

"You've got the main lodge, cabins, pool house, massage cabin, main desk with fishing shop—and no driving inside the compound. Except for me." No grin. Kurt nodded at his shiny black F-250 pickup parked in the road. It had a metal rack over the back with a ladder tied down, and a sliding flat cover over the bed. "The way Mr. Den wants it. He figured the bikes would give kind of a Crested Butte townie feel, I guess. The guests love them. We sell 'em, you wouldn't believe how many. Pink, green, and blue."

"Huh. They take them on the plane?"

"Oh, we ship 'em for two hundred dollars. I mean, they could get one off Amazon for half the price, but they want the actual bike they used here. So that every time their ass hits the seat it reminds them of . . ." He waved again. "This." Kurt lifted one side of his mouth into a half smile. "You'll get used to it."

Jack had a topper on his truck covering the bed and Kurt reached for the latch on the back and Jack put a hand on his arm. "I got this," he said. "Thanks."

Kurt stepped back. "Suit yourself. See you in a couple of hours. Did I say it's a mile and a half of river? You, Cody, the guests, that's it. Me, if I ever have time, which, sad to say, I don't. Mr. Den doesn't even want the cooks or waitstaff or maintenance fishing. Most pristine water on the planet, what he says. We don't ever mention the dam or the reservoir up below the pass. Never mention it. In Mr. Den's mind, in the guests' minds, this is the wildest river on earth. Got it?" Now, finally, a spark of irony flashed in his eyes.

"Yep."

"So our stretch starts at the first big meadow up top, down to the barbed wire at Ellery's. I think you'll have time to scout most of it before dinner. The rest you can fake it."

Jack gave him a thumbs-up.

"When you're fishing upstream, don't go one step past the post at the start of the meadow. There's a sign on it, 'Don't Get Shot!' Not kidding. I think Kreutzer's got a goddamn spotting scope and I know he has a rifle. One day he's gonna kill somebody. No shit."

"Damn."

"I told you: crazy. Batshit crazy."

Kurt turned away, and Jack said, "Oh hey." The manager half turned back. "It's mid-season. What happened to the other guide. My predecessor?"

Kurt's eyes sparked and he pursed his lips. "Predecessor?" He gave Jack a once-over, as if really seeing him for the first time. Compact, broad-shouldered, strung together with maybe baling wire. Whiff of the ranch. Crow's feet at the corners of Jack's eyes earned probably in the saddle, just a guess. Tough. But he'd read on the short résumé "Dartmouth College." Explained the vocabulary. He'd hired college boys before, nothing against them.

"Ken? Ken the Hen. He up and quit. Said it was family trouble but I just don't think he had the stamina." Kurt's smile was straight across. "I knew I needed you two weeks ago, it's getting so damn busy. Now I'm gonna have to get one more."

"Stamina?" Jack said. Guiding was guiding as far as Jack was concerned. It was long days, sometimes a lot of rowing or wading and more or less untangling, more or less retying on lost flies, more or less encouragement depending on the client, but . . .

"You know how much it costs to stay here?" Kurt wasn't looking at him but at maybe a beetle on the ground. "Didn't think so. Well, the folks who stay here are a different breed." The manager rubbed his forehead with three fingers under the brim of his hat, settled the Resistol back on sweat-plastered hair, and nodded once. He walked around Jack's truck and down the smooth track to his own rig. He had a slight hitch, probably from some old injury. The road was covered in pine needles and they crunched under his boots.

•

August. Best time of year to fish. From now straight through September.

He didn't need to be on the ranch. Pop would be all right . . . when wasn't he? Jack had helped his father put up most of the hay. They'd had no rain or major breakdowns and Pop had insisted he take off. After haying, there wasn't much else to do except fix stuff . . . which Pop did can't-see to can't-see every day. Fences, machinery, pumps, trailers, trucks. He never stopped. Jack wondered if it had been different when his mother was alive. She had died in a horse accident when he was eleven. Could it have been fourteen years ago? Had Pop worked himself that hard for that long? Jack wondered if his parents had ever just sat and watched the running clouds or taken a nap. Jack honestly couldn't recall. They must have. But he remembered clearly the sense of the love between them, almost like something on the air, a scent, or a stirring as a breeze stirs, and he remembered their laughter. He figured that to foster a love like that they must have taken the time to enjoy each other and the world.

This year, there'd been plenty of snowpack and the cows were up loose in the mountains and the browse was rich. If the autumn snow held off, he could guide here through the season and help Pop gather the herd at the end of October. His father liked to wait until after the first blizzard anyway; he said that the cows were much easier to convince. Jack thought he just liked riding across slopes softened with snow and striped with the blue shadows of aspen, when the dry powder shook off his chaps like dust.

He and Pop rode on the slopes of Sheep Mountain mostly, where you could break out into a sage meadow and look north to the Never Summers or south to the Gore Range shimmering in snowy brilliance. Usually it was just Pop and he and the dogs, but sometimes Uncle Lloyd rode with them, and sometimes Willy came up from Granby. His border collies were hellacious workers, even Chica, who was barely a pup. They had fun. Jack liked the hard smells of winter woods—ice riming the blowdown branches, the cold stones of the creeks—and the sounds: bit-ring jangle, knock of a hoof, occasional bellow of a panicked cow, the distant whistles of Willy and Pop working the dogs. He liked the steam of the horses' breath when they rode up in the first light. It was one of his favorite things on earth and he stood now at the back of his truck and stopped thinking about it because he didn't like the clench in his heart.

He closed his eyes. He smelled the warm pine needles on the sandy track and heard the muffled rush of the river reverberating in its bed and murmured, "You're all right. New gig, couple months, knee deep in a river. What could be better?" And he almost believed it.

CHAPTER ONE

That first afternoon he dumped his duffel and pack on the rag rug in the cabin and changed fast into nylon shorts. He put a packet of split shot and a small fly box in the breast pockets of his shirt, then pulled the five-weight Winston rod out of the truck and pieced it together. His wading boots were drying in the back seat and he tugged on wool socks and laced the boots, and slung over his head the lanyard that dangled nippers, tippet, forceps, Gink. It was just warm enough and he liked best to go without waders. The water would be icy but he was on his own: he wouldn't have to stand in the water for hours beside a casting client. He'd be moving fast.

He did. He began at the big dark sliding pool below the cabin and worked upstream. He could see a hatch of mayflies coming off the slow water beside the shore. Blue-winged olives. He always loved how they rose from an eddy in deep shadow like animated snowflakes and flew up into sunlight and flared in a haze of soft sparks. He crouched on the bank and turned over a rock the size of a brick in the shallows and the silted underside was covered with the pupae of caddis, almost like a crusting of cloves. A stone fly also crawled over the cobble in the unexpected air. Due diligence. He'd fished the mountains of Colorado all his life, and he had a good idea what bugs would be where. He tied on a dry and a dropper, a tufty elk hair stimulator on top and a bead-head pheasant tail on the bottom. Clients loved fishing this rig and he did, too.

He stepped into the icy water, caught his breath at the first clinch of cold. And then he waded in up to his knees and began to cast.

•

The rhythm of it always soothed him. Laying the line out straight over dark water, the blip of the weighted dropper, the dry fly touching just after, the—

The tuft of elk hair barely touched and the surface broke. The lightest tug and he set the hook and the rod bent and quivered and a colossal brown trout leapt clear of the water into a spray of sunlight. Jesus. It splashed down and ran straight upstream and he let the fish take the line to the reel and he heard the whir of the clicking drag and he ran after it. He splashed through shallows, slipped, stumbled, half his body in the water, didn't care if he spooked everyone in the big pool. Somehow he tightened down the drag knob on the reel just a little as he went—it was sleek this brown, all muscle, and the flash of gold as it hit the air was better than any treasure, God. He ran and fought the fish. Ten minutes, twenty? Who knew. He lost track of time, and of himself. Forgot it was he, Jack, who fished, whose limbs and hands acted without thought. He forgot his name or that he owned one, and for the first time in many months he was as close as he could come to something like joy.

He was almost under the bridge when he raised the rod high and brought the exhausted trout in the last few feet and unshucked the net from his belt and slid it under this beauty and cradled her in the mesh. She was a species of gold that no jeweler had ever encountered—deeper, darker, rich with tones that had depth like water. He talked to her the whole time, *You're all right, you're all right, thank you, you beauty,* almost as he had talked to himself at the shack, and he wet his left hand and cupped her belly gently and slipped the barbless hook from her lip and withdrew the net.

He crouched with the ice water to his hips and held her quietly into the current until half his body was numb. Held and held her who knew how long and watched her gills work, and she mostly floated free between his guiding fingers, and he felt the pulsing touch of her flanks as her tail worked and she idled. And then she wriggled hard and darted and he lost her shape to the green shadows of the stones.

Thank you, he said again after her but it was not so much said as an emotion released—released like the fish to the universe. He straightened. He was almost under the plank-and-timber bridge and he looked up and he saw the camera.

•

It was a black fish-eye lens fixed to the main beam. A half bubble three inches across. Glassy like nothing else out here, inanimate and silent. Was someone watching him? Should he be bothered? He was. Kurt hadn't mentioned any cameras. He splashed his face and glanced up at it again. Was it menacing? It was just a camera. But he felt violated. Because he had so given himself—to the river, the fish, the first afternoon on a new stretch of water—because he had, for the first time maybe since the death of his friend Wynn, allowed himself to feel a shiver of peace. He was pissed that he had thought himself completely alone and someone might have witnessed it all.

Fuck it. He had his hand half-lifted to give the camera the finger, but stopped himself. Whoever might be on the other end, he didn't want to give them the satisfaction. He waded back to the far shore, ducked under the bridge, and fished on. A kingfisher dropped from a limb above him and swooped upstream to the next perch and kept him company. And he didn't have to look back to know there was another lens on the upstream side of the bridge.

•

He fished. He was in no hurry now. He didn't care if he was in time to chat it up with the guests, or meet the other guide, or the staff. He fished with the evening sun on his back, and around the tight bend, south, into shadow. Fuck 'em. Maybe not the best attitude for a new job.

But the fishing was a separate thing, as if the spilling river and the breezy afternoon could not be stained. They couldn't. Around the bend was another long riffle with a scattering of boulders, and low ledges foaming into smooth black pools and he could see why fishers went crazy. There were still a couple of hours of good daylight and he had to make himself turn around.

•

He was back at the cabin at 6:05 and he rinsed in the hot shower, put on jeans and boots and a snap shirt, and coasted the teal bike down to the main lodge at 6:20. The clouds had cleared, it would be a cold night, and they already had a fire roaring in the stone hearth. Overkill, Jack thought; it might be sixty degrees outside. To the left of the fireplace were half a dozen tables, four of which were set for dinner. A swing door with a little window led from the dining area to what must be the kitchen. To the right of the hearth was a U-shaped mahogany bar where five people sat on stools, and a tall broad-shouldered Brit with shaggy blond hair presided behind it. Ginnie the Enforcer. Two-Drink Ginnie. He knew she was a Brit because she called, "Ahh, come on in, mate. We've been expecting you. You've barely got time . . ." And he heard the sigh of a cap being cracked and she set a sweating bottle on a napkin on the polished wood, Cutthroat ale. "Come in, don't be shy. Everyone, this is Jack. Jack, Everyone. Have a seat." The conversation stopped and Everyone turned on their stools.

"Scooch a bit closer, love," Ginnie said to Jack, and she raised a no-touch thermometer from behind the bar.

•

Suddenly staying at home and working the ranch with a taciturn father was looking more appealing. It was the second time in a few hours that Jack had been set back on his heels. Ginnie was exuberant, she had little use for polite preliminaries, she left no room for second thoughts. He got it. In this way she was the perfect maître d'hôtel of a rustic getaway for the rich and famous. Once the guests got used to her provincial pub manners they were at ease in a way that was probably refreshing. Ginnie blew zero smoke and didn't give a shit what was in your portfolio or how many gold records you had made. *Was the fishing good? Was it fun anyway? Did you see the bald eagle in the big aspen right over the trout pond? Did you know that he ate their precious stocked trout like popcorn? That you couldn't shoot the sonofabitch because he's federally protected?*

"I wish I were federally protected. Can you imagine? Hand over all your large bills and see you tomorrow! Ha!" She was a hoot, he got it. She also seemed to know just when to dial it back. She must have noticed his discomfort as he pulled up a stool, because she stuck out an elbow to bump, and in a calm, confiding tone, she said, "I'm Ginnie. Glad you're here," and she smiled a real, almost shy smile. "I know my reputation precedes me, but I'm not that strict. Kurt means well. Tell me where you're coming from, love."

And in that way she slipped him into a bubble of conversation in which he did not have to meet the guests all at once, and she slid him a jar of long beef jerky twists, the real stuff, made from strips of sirloin probably, and crusted with pepper, and she said, "Eat as many as you like but save your appetite, Gionno has made his famous elk loin tonight."

In a few minutes, he had acclimated enough to introduce himself to the others—Alison K, early thirties, who was famous but who had creases at the corners of her eyes and an air of someone in the habit of pursuing truth; she was seated next to a large man, heavyset with dark combed-back hair, who wore a blue sport coat and a pinky ring; he glanced at Jack, swept him up and down with dour eyes, nodded, no fist bump or name. Next to him was Will in a silver-buttoned vest and ostrich boots, maybe sixty, clearly well-heeled, and his wife (?), Neave, forty-ish, with turquoise earrings and the most luxurious black hair halfway down her back; a younger couple in their late twenties, in Arc'teryx fleece and moccasins, who Jack bet were accomplished fisherpeople and who had probably already thrown flies on every continent. And Cody, the other guide—lean, maybe six feet, three-day beard, high cheeks, and eyes set wide like a wolf's—who was too far around the bar to shake hands. But when the dinner bell did chime, and they all stood, and he and Cody met by the hearth and shook—the handshake an F-you to the virus—Jack noticed his White's packer boots, and felt in the iron grip and calloused fingers the temper of another ranch kid. Cody's eyes when they met his were not friendly or unfriendly, just watchful. Fair enough.

•

He and Cody shared a table in the far corner, downstream, beside a window that overlooked the river. In the long silences they ate with a sharp hunger and Cody raised a finger to Shay, the server, twice, and she picked up his plate and brought it back heaped with elk loin and gravy and mashed potatoes.

"You can do that?" Jack murmured. "Get seconds or thirds?"

"Eat as much as you want."

"Damn."

"You'll get used to it." The second time he'd heard the phrase that day.

Jack ate and looked out the French window and watched the river fill up with shadow and watched the low sun burnish the tops of the tallest pines.

"Did you fish it?" Cody said.

"Huh? Sorry . . ."

Shay set down two dessert plates, panna cotta with fresh blue-berries. She stepped back quickly as if she'd just fed two lions. "Three-two-one go!" she said. "No seconds," she added, "but I do have tons of ice cream." Jack thought her accent was Carolinas somewhere. She wore tight jeans and a light plaid shirt and had a simple small anchor tattoo on the inside of a wrist, maybe homemade.

Cody actually smiled, first one Jack had seen. "Ain't gonna bite," he said to Shay.

"TBD," she said, and went back through the swinging door.

Jack said, "Sorry, you were asking."

"Did you have time to fish before dinner?"

"Oh, yeah, I did."

Cody slipped his spoon into the flank of the panna cotta, didn't look up. "Which way?"

"Upstream."

"The pool under the bridge."

"Yep."

"Get to the post?"

"I saw the meadow, turned around."

Cody didn't say another word. He ate his dessert and lifted a chin at Shay, who came through the door with a silver cof-feepot. "Really?" she said as she sailed by. "Ice cream? Gee, I wouldn't have guessed. Jack?" Jack shook his head.

On her way back Shay filled their coffee cups. They both drank it black. "What's with the cameras?" Jack said finally.

Cody was studiously corralling blueberries with his spoon, tongue in the corner of his mouth like he was solving a math problem. He glanced up. "Cameras?"

"Yeah, on the bridge."

"Dude lives in England. Mr. Den. Most of the year. He likes to watch the trout under the bridge. The salmon when they're running."

"Huh. Bet he likes to see who's fishing, too."

Cody shrugged. "He knows your face. Knew it before you got here. No alarm bells there."

"Any other cameras? I mean on the river."

Cody gave up and tilted the blueberries on the plate into his palm and ate the whole bunch. His wolf eyes never changed. No light there, really, no passing shadows, just a flat watchfulness. "Never seen any. The one who's probably got cameras is Kreutzer. I wouldn't take a half step beyond his line. He shot at me last summer, no shit. I don't know if he missed or he's just a really good shot."

"Damn."

"Dicey around here. Downstream? Past the wire? Ellery doesn't shoot, he just has dogs."

"Dogs? Mr. Jensen didn't mention any dogs."

"He wouldn't. I guess he figures he'll ease you in. Make sure you don't get shot first, tell you about mauling later."

"Damn. What kind of dogs?"

"Mastiffs, hounds. Like five of 'em. And a couple of German shepherds. They chase deer. Once in a while they'll drag one back. Never seen anything like it."

"Whoa."

"Mauled a fisherman in June. Nearly killed him."

"They weren't put down?"

"Guy had a Glock in his vest. Armed intruder was how Ellery framed it. Had the right to self-defense. DA went along with it. Not sure why the dude didn't get the gun out fast enough."

Jack knew why. Mastiffs, unlike most other dogs, will some-times silently stalk their prey. Probably leapt on the poor bas-tard mid-cast, the way a lion would.

"Jesus," Jack said. "Fishing around here is high stakes."

Cody's laugh was short, more like a cough, and joyless.

Jack sipped his coffee. He noticed that Cody picked up his cup in two hands, the way you would at a fire on a cold night. Hunter for sure, rancher almost certainly. Jack said, "You all run cows? You and your folks?"

For the first time Cody's eyes darkened. "Folks passed."

"I'm sorry." Jack was about to say that his own mother had gone many years before but he closed his mouth.

"We did run cattle," Cody said. "The Flying W. Dad had a little airstrip."

"Where at?"

"Hotchkiss."

Jack nodded. He knew the country. He and Pop and Uncle Lloyd had hunted units in the West Elks a couple of years for a change of scenery.

End of conversation, apparently. Shay brought a soda fountain glass stuffed with three scoops of chocolate ice cream and Cody dug in. Jack excused himself. "Been a long day," he said. "I better get sorted."

He passed the table where Alison K ate with the man in the jacket and she looked up, smiled, said, "See you bright and early."

"Yes, ma'am." He touched the brim of his baseball cap and pushed out through the heavy door into the cold night.

•

Sky deep with stars and the smells of coming fall stirring up the river. Might even frost before morning. He rolled the bike off its kickstand and walked it up the smooth track. Just up the hill was a grove of aspen and their leaves ticked and rustled in a brief wave as a breeze came through. In the morning he'd encourage Alison K to linger over her coffee, maybe they'd talk about hatches and flies and strategies in the sun on the porch while they'd wait for the water to warm a little. Many fishers thought the earlier the better, thought daybreak was best. On the salt, maybe, in the ocean; but in the mountains the insects hatched when the day warmed, and trout were a little like people: they liked to wake up and get stirring before they ate breakfast.

•

That night he was uneasy. He cracked the windows and turned the black thermostat on the wall to off and started a fire in the woodstove. More for the flutter of flames and the popping aspen than for the heat. A fire was good company. He tugged his sleeping bag out of its stuff sack and laid it over the blankets. Did he feel claustrophobic? How could he? He could hear the river through the open windows, intermittent, almost like breathing. And it was his favorite kind of stream, a mountain creek, really, coursing through rockfall, pushing gravel bars up into the insides of the bends, sifting through blowdown. The best kind of water in the world to walk and wade and cast as you went. And it flowed through the sweetest cut. The canyon brimmed with pines and spruce and scattered aspen, and broken sandstone up high, and there was nothing above the bands of rimrock but higher mountains, the Beckwiths and Raggeds.

And above those a felted blackness, limitless, and dense with stars. What could be better? It was his mantra, what he told himself again and again as he went through his day and tried to keep his eyes clear and his heart open. If not open, at least strong—his spirit. *What could be better?*

But he did feel closed in. He remembered the same sensation during his first weeks at college in New Hampshire—the relentless woods, the private property and fences everywhere, the narrow views of the sky. It took him a while back then to discern the particular beauty of northern New England, the more intimate expanses, the pockets of true wildness.

CHAPTER TWO

That night he dreamt of Wynn. They were fishing a creek together, a creek out of some myth that ran in a braid of silver between two countries: one burned to black, black earth blown with swirls of ash, black stumps charred to daggers and still smoking. And on the other side green woods, lush with late summer, and along the banks tall grass and pink fireweed, the swaying limbs of spruce, and birdsong. The stream ran like a shining cord between them and they were fishing it together. They fished it the way they always did, he wading higher into virgin water, casting up into the bends, and Wynn coming a ways behind, taking his time, pool to pool, managing to catch just as many trout though Jack had already fished through. Too far apart to talk but close enough to hail.

In the dream the burned country was on his right as he pushed upstream, and the current was cold and alive against his un-wadered legs, the wind cooling the backs of his ears, and he turned once and saw Wynn casting across, the tall length of him leaning a little, the verdant trees behind and above him. The way he moved: the back cast with the sure rhythm of a metronome but easy, too, the line whispering out straight, and Jack knew in the next moment Wynn would be on a fish. And in the dream he turned away with a kind of tact, to give his friend the privacy of the catch without audience, and he waded up into his own riffle and continued to cast.

He dropped the dry fly at the edge of the far bank to mimic a bug falling out of the grass and saw a huge fish break water and even before he felt the sharp pull of the line he turned for a split second to celebrate with Wynn and Wynn was gone. An upstream wind blew a gust of ash across the pool and there was no Wynn in the drifting plume. Jack's rod was jumping and the reel was unspooling but he dropped it and ran, straight into the bitter grit of the cloud, but even as he did he knew he would never see his chosen brother again. He knew he would stand in the icy current and the ash would dust the black water and he would call and call and there would never be an answer. In all that divided country he would be alone.

He woke sometime in the middle of the night and his pillow was wet and he did not have to remind himself that the scene was not at all a myth, that the very stream existed, far to the north, and that it was probably running this very night between acrid char and rustling woods and that Wynn's spirit might be there, too. Hovering where three years before Jack had tried to stanch his bleeding.

•

Jack splashed his face in the sink and stepped onto the porch in his boxers. Cold night, nearly frost. The gap in the woods over the river was rashed with stars and he thought they were like the goose bumps spreading over his limbs. No way to shake it, the grief. Or numb it, either, standing nearly naked above the rush of this August creek. *It's mine,* he might have murmured; *mine to carry.*

Wynn's loss reverberated and was swept up into the more pervasive loss of his mother just as the sound of the stream rose up and was scattered by the wind in these pines. *How do you do it?* He asked himself the question all the time. He blamed himself for both deaths. Sometimes he wondered if he should join them.

•

He stood at the edge of the deck and listened to the sounds of water and smelled the breath of the creek, which in its chill carried a portent of fall. He was uneasy. Not just the dream but something about this place. He stepped to the upstream corner of the porch. He crouched and reached to the damp ground and found the rounded cold river rock, and then felt over a foot to the right and dug in the matted needles; he fetched up his keys. People always hid their keys high on a door or window frame, or low under a rock. Nobody just dug them into the duff. He walked barefoot up to his truck and opened the topper and slid out his .30-.30 carbine rifle. When he got back to the cabin he scraped the clinging dirt off his feet on the oak threshold and leaned the rifle in the corner by his bed. That was better.

He lay awake for a while longer thinking about Wynn and his new situation and before he fell asleep he saw through the upstream window a ruddy half-moon rising out of the spindly pines of a high ridge. A dim moon, but waxing, and casting enough light to throw a shadow.

•

How do you do it? . . .

How you do it is have breakfast at seven. Kurt had said that the guests always felt like they were getting their money's worth if they had to wake up at daybreak. Maybe it was like a real ranch. He'd said, "You and I know the good fishing might not start till nine. But you'd be surprised. Shay has the coffeepot in the lodge ready at six, in the dark, and the fire going, and I shit you not, a lot of the guests will be right there. On the feedback forms many say it was their favorite part of the day. Drinking coffee and watching the day break. Like they had to come way up here to learn how to do it."

Well, it was Jack's, too—favorite time. He didn't want to make conversation that early, though, so he'd make his first cup of coffee here at the cabin. He had the fixings in his truck.

•

He walked down to the lodge with his pack and waders and one rod at 6:50. Alison K had told him at the bar the night before that she had her own outfit, waders, boots, vest, and would use her own Scott five weight. Fine with Jack. He had extra gear and so did the lodge, but clients were very particular.

He set his pack on the porch and another of his own rods in its tube strapped to the side of it. *Remember to get the snacks,* he told himself. The jerky and cookies, cans of pop and water bottles Kurt had said Shay would have ready for them. They'd fish all morning and come back to the lodge for lunch and then fish again, either right away or in the evening, depending on Ms. K's preference.

Alison K was standing at the blazing hearth with a mug of coffee when he entered. She was alone. He could see through the French windows the younger fleecy couple out on the deck overlooking the river; there was a hearth out there, too, and the flames were blowing around in the downstream wind. They stood by the fire but a table was set. Huh. Pretty cold still, nearly a frost. Jack had slept more nights out under the stars than he could count, and made more breakfasts over an open fire in every kind of weather, but he didn't think he'd choose to eat out there when there was a warm room inside. He didn't see the super-rich couple. He wasn't sure why he was calling them that in his head.

Alison K was wearing workout tights, a dun-colored mohair sweater, and a baseball cap that said HOMER TACKLE AND SUPPLY above the brim. Inconspicuous silver earrings. She turned and smiled and he nodded and went on to the side table in the dining room where coffeepots were labeled French Roast Dark, Yergachef Light, and Costa Rican Decaf. He poured a cup of the dark and hesitated and came back. He didn't want to intrude.

"Ma'am," he said. "Morning."

"Good morning, Jack. It's Jack, right?"

He nodded.

"Is it short for anything? Jackson or John or Jonathan?"

He shook his head. "Nope," he said. "My parents were too wary."

"Wary?"

"Of diminutives, I guess."

Her eyes flickered and she gave him an up-and-down, reassessing maybe.

"I mean, they would've had a heart attack if teachers at school started calling me Johnny."

Now she laughed. It surprised her and her hand shook and she almost spilled her coffee. "Right," she said. "Mine weren't so savvy. I got called Ally."

"Life can be hard."

She studied Jack again. His humor was drier than dry, the way she liked it most. "If you call me Ally we won't get along."

"Got it."

Someone came out of the kitchen, the young woman from last night, and chimed the bell hanging on the wall. Shay—that was her name. Alison K said, "Care to join me for breakfast, Jack-not-Johnny?"

"I thought you might be eating with your friend."

"He's not my friend. I mean he is. His name is Vincent and he's head of my . . ." She hesitated. "Security. He insists on casing every place I stay for more than a night. God." She smiled as if the thought of Vincent gave her real pleasure. "He means well. The manager, Mr. Jensen, was not at all happy about it."

Jack nodded. "Is it allowed? Me eating breakfast with you? It's my first day, I don't know all the rules."

"Doesn't strike me that either of us ever really gave a damn about rules anyway. C'mon."

•

Ham-and-egg scramble, home fries, Belgian waffles with real maple syrup and whipped cream. Homemade sourdough, Cabot cheddar. The plates came out at a brisk pace. They ate in avid silence for a while, making small animal sounds, and then she said,

"Not local, are you?"

His mouth was full. He pointed out the windows, across the river, and gave his finger a double pump, as if to say, *Some distance north, over those mountains.* As he did he saw that Cody had joined the couple at their outdoor table. Good, he was eating with his clients, too.

"Colorado?" she said.

He washed down some waffle with a slug of coffee. "Yep, near Kremmling."

"What happens in Kremmling?"

"Sunrise, elk migration. Stuff like that."

"Mountains?"

"Never Summers and the Gore Range."

"God, the names. You could almost walk into the words them-selves." Now Jack put down his cup. He'd never heard anyone say that and it was true. For a moment he lost the blithe tempo of their conversation that had shielded him from his own shy-ness. For just a second he was at his own kitchen table back home, looking through the big window from which he could see both ranges. He felt his eyes moisten. She was tactful and half turned away and motioned to Shay for more coffee.

"Cattle at home, too. Right?" she said after their cups had been refilled.

"Yes."

"Thought so. Family ranch?"

He nodded. Was he that obvious? Well, he'd sussed Cody from the get-go. "Pop and me."

"Do you mind if I ask what happened to Mom? Am I being too nosy?"

"It's all right. She died in a horse accident when I was eleven."

"Oh. Ow. I'm so sorry."

"Thank you."

"I lost my father when I was fourteen. I grew up in the mountains, too. North Carolina."

What he liked, thinking about it later, was the ease with which she shifted gears. She was playful and game, but her repartee was always respectful, and when there was something true or beautiful to reckon with she slowed way down and considered.

They didn't talk once about politics or sports or the sickness. The novel virus from three years before that kept mutating, the superbug that finally broke out of India. But Jack knew that there was a reason the very rich preferred to spend their vacations now deep in the mountains, in regions where the viruses were still rare.

•

They geared up in the slanting sun on the front porch. He had guided many fishers who thought it was a race to get on the water. As if getting into waders, boots, stringing line, tying on tippet and flies were all something to get over with at a hundred miles an hour. As if getting on the water ten minutes sooner meant catching more fish. But somehow it never did.

He liked to take his time and it was evident that she did, too. He had always found that the rhythm of fishing—the patient, music-like rhythm one needed—began with slipping the rod sections out of their flannel wrapping, with holding each to the light, with stretching the leader properly between sliding fingers that burned with the friction of the line. Each step given its due. Often he caught himself humming. It was the same relaxed pace that allowed one to step into the current and carefully consider the patterns of rock and pool, current, shadow, wind that went into the unconscious calculus of every cast. Start too fast and you'd stumble and hack your way into the morning. He'd done it too many times as a kid, and so the slower pacing was not inherited but learned.

It was clear that she was not at all green and had learned it, too. And she was humming. In a husky, sweet voice that he recognized but couldn't place. Sometimes she sang a snatch of song, barely above a whisper, and he was sure he'd heard it on the radio.

"How do you feel about a dry and dropper?" he said from one of the Adirondack chairs where he was lacing up his wading boots.

"What I'm most used to," she said.

"Okay, great. We'll tie on when we get down there." She nodded and took off her cap and shook out her hair, which was thick and ruddy brown in the new sunlight, nearly the copper color of spruce bark. She regathered it behind her and slipped it more snugly through the hair band and worked it again through the baseball cap. "Ready," she said. But he had already made himself look away.

•

Jack was twenty-five. He'd been in love once, but then again he sometimes wondered if that were true. He'd known Cheryl since second grade, since her father had come to Grand County to be the police chief of Granby. Over the years in a small school, they'd been adversaries, buddies, embarrassed spin-the-bottle kissers. She was a fine equestrian and she had helped him and his dad search for missing cows on the mountain more than once. And then, junior year she had come over one afternoon to help him train his new filly, Cassie. It was early September and hot, and she had Cassie on the lunge line in the sun and dust for over an hour. The four-year-old was remarkably patient and clearly wanting to please, responding as well as she could to the gentle commands to change gait—neck rounded, ear closest to the girl twitching to her low voice, chest dark with sweat. And Jack knew it was her energy—Cheryl's—that the young horse could feel. It was the way this girl with the lanky frame and dark bob encouraged everyone, her generosity and seriousness.

He leaned against the rail of the corral and marveled and admitted to himself that he wasn't worth crap as a horse trainer. Afterward they decided to ride down to the river and cool off. They brought lead ropes from the barn and he whistled in Duke and Mindy and they slipped on the halters and then swung up and rode them without saddles or bridles along the east edge of the big hay meadow to the river. They rode into the shade of a huge cottonwood and swung down. The swimming hole was a slow blackwater pool above a natural ledge-rock weir and Jack always felt cooler just hearing the current sift through the drop.

They tied the horses and stripped to their underwear and jumped in. And yelled with the shock. And clambered back out onto the bank almost as fast, and into the spontaneous silence of another shock: blinking in the dappled light, soaked, goosebumped, in wet skivvies that now hid nothing, they saw in each other a young man and a young woman, full-fledged and glorious. And they laughed—discomfort, surprise, and joy all together—and somehow ended in each other's arms.

Over the next two years they were rarely apart. In late fall she rode up into the Never Summers with Jack and his father and the dogs to gather part of the herd. She hunted with Jack in November and they camped above Harrier Basin in the snow and built a blazing fire outside their tarp lean-to and stayed up much too late playing dominoes and trying to devise ways to toast and ruin every marshmallow in the bag Jack had packed as a treat. When she, not Jack, shot the cow elk for the one tag they'd drawn, they quartered it together, hide on, and tied two quarters each with baling twine and slung them over their saddles, hide to leather, and walked the horses out to the truck. They rode back up the next morning to break down the camp and decided to skip school and stay an extra two nights. Jack thought it was a spontaneous decision but found out later she'd already told her father they'd be gone.

In this way—the way she trained her horses—she loved Jack into some semblance of comfort in opening a heart that had closed since the death of his mother. This was precocious for a sixteen-year-old, the work of a young woman, really, not a girl, and she enacted it with patience.

Jack had already kept mostly to himself outside of school. Since his mother died he had shied from team sports, which he thought were exhibitionist and encouraged the worst kind of cocky behavior. His mother was gone because he had gotten too big for his britches. Too many nights he dreamt it: a summer morning on the Encampment, riding on a narrow high trail above the roaring gorge—Pop going first, leading his skittish packhorse, then Mom on sweet Mindy, and then he on Duke bringing up the rear. Because he had insisted; because he thought he was big enough now at eleven.

He knew it was his own cockiness that had caused her to die. And so he had withdrawn from group activities into helping Pop with the ranch, and reading. He read and read with the hunger of someone seeking more than diversion. And had gotten used to taking long rides on Duke by himself, and losing himself with a fly rod on the river and in the mountain creeks.

So it was not a huge adjustment to make room for another. Cheryl rode as easily as she walked. She did not fish but was happy collecting stones and studying tracks. She liked a good story and so did not mind reading. At sixteen, the two were nearly inseparable, and all of junior and senior years they lived almost as if they were married. They were not allowed to spend the night together at either house, but their three collective parents were wise enough to know that water flows downhill, and so they allowed themselves to believe that their afternoons together and the increasingly frequent camping trips were merely the extension of a childhood friendship.

Did Jack miss her? Sometimes. But at some point he had to admit that he loved the memories more than their time together. She got less and less interested in anything but studying hard and spending time with him, and she was so serious. In April of their senior year she got into CSU pre-vet, and he into Dartmouth, and she begged him to consider staying in Colorado. She wanted to get married and raise a family and she knew they could do it at some point in their studies. They could handle it. But he had begun to feel a constriction in his spirit when he was around her, and in his second year of college away in New Hampshire he had to admit that a future with Cheryl felt more like a tunnel than an adventure and he wrote her the letter.

•

"Hey, guru," he heard Alison say. "We going fishing or what?"

Jack shook himself. He was not on the ranch back home but here, in a chair, in the sun. *Stay present, dude, Jesus.* "Oh, yeah, sorry."

She was holding her rod and smiling with whimsy, almost as if she knew. When she smiled the crow's feet deepened at the corners of her eyes. She was fully dressed in waders with a tight webbing belt to keep water out of the legs in case of a fall. She wore her own vest. "Ready," he said. "Let's hit it."

He slung the pack, shoved the long-handled net into the back of his own belt, and they stepped into the shade of the trail that led down the bank to the river.

CHAPTER THREE

At lunch Kurt, the manager, pulled him aside.

He and Alison K had fished for three hours straight. They had walked down the good trail to Ellery's wire fence—no killer dogs in sight—and had worked upstream just to the bottom of the big pool below his cabin. She was a competent fisher with a smooth cast and didn't mind wading in stiff current. She had a sense of humor about her screw-ups and was eager for any instruction and critique. He'd shown her how to lift the rod fast and skip the fish over the surface to net it, and how to lay out successive mends in a stiff current. He'd demonstrated the long cast and she'd mimicked him. She yelped at every hit, and she must have hooked on to a dozen fish and brought in most of them. He'd stopped counting. The plan was to continue up under the bridge to the meadow in the afternoon.

The day had warmed and a table had been set for them in the sun on the outdoor deck. No hearth fire needed. Shay had offered them local farm-to-table roast beef and heirloom tomato sandwiches on homemade rye. And sweet sun tea. No objections. He didn't see either the Youngens—the fleecy couple—or Silver Buttons and his wife. Jack had pulled out his chair and was about to sit down when the big man creaked the boards of the steps.

"Don't mean to interrupt," Kurt said, touching his spotless fawn cowboy hat.

"Not at all," Alison K said. "Would you like to join us?" She was lit from the morning and feeling expansive. "We can pull up another chair, plenty of room."

"Ate earlier, thank you. Jack, a quick word."

Jack followed his boss inside the lodge, where they stood by the now empty bar. "Did you hear the news?" Kurt said.

"News? There's no signal in my cabin, no wireless, no cell. When I drove in yesterday my radio went to snow as soon as I hit the canyon."

Kurt nodded. "They confirmed a case of the virus in town this morning."

"Crested Butte?"

Kurt nodded. "We're encouraging our staff not to drive in. Can't prevent you, but it's unwise. The patient 'Y' is in quarantine at the hospital in Gunnison. Another case or three and the government will lock down the town. The way they did up in Rawlins."

"Huh."

"All the guests are booked for the entire ten days, so that's a good thing. By then if there's no new cases it should quiet down."

Jack was suddenly thinking of his father and of home. "Any word on any other towns?"

"Nope, CB was all I heard. Okay, just thought I'd tell ya. No reason to share it with the guests. Not a thing we can do about it and they come for peace and quiet."

"Right," Jack said slowly.

"Thanks." Kurt squeezed his shoulder with a hand like a vise grip and tightened his mouth into something like a grin. "She do good this morning?"

"Yes."

"Good. She had that air." Kurt released his hand, turned away, turned back. "Oh, one more thing."

Jack waited.

"Ana, the gal that cleans, was tidying your cabin and saw the thirty-thirty in the corner. It frightened her."

The aggravation that had coiled when the man had touched him now rose like a snake into Jack's chest.

"I didn't ask anyone to clean up after me."

Kurt stretched his mouth into a thin line. Meant to be a smile maybe, but his eyes were hard. "Cowboy through and through. Well, if that's what you want. She means well. You can leave your bedclothes and towels on the porch on Sundays. 'Less you want to wash 'em in the creek. Ha!"

Jack didn't say anything.

"But anyway, we don't allow firearms on the premises. Like I said, the guests come for peace and quiet and they can get mighty touchy. Just a policy of Mr. Den's. So when you're done tonight you can bring whatever you have up to the gun room in the office. Good with you?"

No, not really. "I'll bring it along," Jack said. The .30-.30 was Jack's saddle gun, the classic lever-action carbine made famous in every western. Iron sights, no scope, short and light. It was easy to carry, easy to swing, and sighted in dead-on at a hundred yards. He didn't tell Kurt that he had a Glock 26 in his fishing waist pack. He wasn't a gun nut, he was just a fisher and a hunter who spent a lot of time in the mountains.

"Good, thanks. Hope you all do good this afternoon."

And now the manager headed for the heavy front doors but it was Jack who stopped him. "Mr. Jensen?"

"Yeah?" Kurt was irritated. Well, so was Jack.

"I never saw Cody on the river this morning. Didn't they fish?"

"He drove 'em out to Tomichi Creek," Kurt said. "We have rights there, too." He shoved out the door.

Jack stood in the dim bar and wondered also why Mr. Silver Buttons and his wife didn't seem to have been assigned a guide.

•

Jack put the manager out of his mind, or tried. But it wasn't until they were through lunch and back on the creek that his anger swirled away in the thigh-deep current. The thing about fishing: it washed everything away but water and stone and wind. And bird cry. And blowdown. And a spiderweb's gleamings in the exposed roots of a cut bank. And in a tailwater pool: the spreading rings of rising trout, dapping silently like slow rain. His heart rose to these things like a hungry fish and he could forget himself. It was why, after his mother died, he disappeared into the creeks. The only place aside from books he could find a minute of solace.

Usually he was alone, but he had guided on and off since he was sixteen and he liked it, as long as he wasn't with a total ass. And if he was with someone like Alison K it was fun and he could lose himself in her own absorption.

She knew how to be absorbed. That was something else Jack had noticed about people who had attained mastery in a chosen discipline—that ability to be immersed. Focus was one thing, and necessary, but it was active. The energy went from the actor to the activity: Okay, I'm casting now, I'll focus on casting. I'm painting, I'll focus on the canvas and the touch of my brush. I'm dancing, I will leap in cascading symmetries. What he'd noticed in all true masters was that the focus turned soon, or immediately, into full absorption by the act itself. The actor surrendered, and it was as if, like a change in tide, the energy was now flowing in the opposite direction—from the river, or the basketball court, or the painting. Flowing into the one who was doing. It swept her up and carried her. It fueled her, and in the most intense moments allowed her to relax.

Alison K was not a master fly fisher but he could see right away that she knew how to lose herself, which was a rare talent. Rarer than it ought to be. When she got on a fish she yelled like she was five. He had caught himself doing it, too.

They decided to drop down the trail right below the lodge and fish upstream from there. They started in full sun and soon they were shucking sweaters down to their base layers. Jack wore a light synthetic hoodie in camo, hood back, and she was in a tight olive Capilene undershirt, long-sleeved to protect her from the sun. He wore only the pack and a small waist bag. She had on an abbreviated vest with six pockets that barely snapped in front, and as the creek was rarely more than crotch deep, she'd folded the bib of her waders down over the belt, as had he. The day was growing hot.

Jack tried to follow the motions of her cast and tried not to notice the length of her neck, the breadth of her shoulders. How gracefully her hands moved, or the thin fabric of her shirt where the vest hid nothing. He made himself concentrate on where she might want guidance. She was lovely and forthright, so what? He thought she was a famous singer but he would never ask.

In the first hour they fished briskly around the bend and to the new water of the long shaded pool below his cabin. They were standing in the shallows and he said, "Hold on. I have an idea."

"You do?" There was so much wry play in the question. Another thing he'd noticed about her: she often let a few words do a lot of work. He was standing just a couple of feet off her left shoulder and he reached for the rod, which she handed to him. On the breeze, barely a breath, he could smell her shampoo and the tang of her sweat.

"There's a hatch of pale morning duns coming off the water. There, just off the bank. The little pale guys."

She didn't say a word, but smiled.

"This pool is easy casting. I just saw a rise, too. Wanna try a straight dry fly? Like an eighteen? They're pretty tiny but you'll see it fine against the dark water."

She was looking at him with unabashed admiration and she nodded, barely. Something about the look: the slow blink, maybe. His heart hammered. He blew out a long cooling breath and said, "Okay," and cradled the rod in his crooked elbow and concentrated on digging the fly box out of his waist pack. "Here it is," he said, and dared to look up.

She was still watching him. Her eyes seemed smoky. "It's okay," she said. "You're a boy and I'm a girl." His mouth must have dropped open because she grinned suddenly and her smile was wide. "But we're fishing. That's what we're doing. I'm having the best time and I'm not a cougar and you're not a sleazebag. So let's keep having a blast."

"Right," he croaked.

•

On her third long cast she made a beautiful throw all the way across the river and six inches upstream from a silently spreading ring; and the hit was so fast and hard, the gulp on the surface so loud they heard it above the current and they both shouted. And the line went taut and the rod tip tugged down hard and quivered and the fight was on. He'd seen the green gold flash of the back only; it was probably a brown and big and it struck in almost the same spot as his beauty from the night before. You couldn't make it up.

The fish ran fast upstream and took her line to the backing on the reel and he shouted, "You gotta run! Can you run after it? Go! Go!"

Her answer was to snug the drag on the reel and wade fast to the bank and go. She was agile. She hopped nimbly from rock to rock, in and out of sunlight. She reeled in line when she could, and she splashed into the water to wade when the fish pulled her in. It had to be a monster. He never saw it. Some fish turned downstream and ballooned open their gills and let the current take them. Not this one. It ran straight into the current. She followed the trout under the bridge and into the next bend, letting it take line as it dashed up the slower runs and zig-zagged in the riffles. He ran after her. At first he called encouragement, a patter of instruction, and then he fell silent. This was all hers and she was meeting it with everything she had.

They rounded a tight bend into deeper shade. The river widened a little into a rocky riffle at the top of which, in sunlight, was the famous post with its sign and the meadow. All on the river's left bank, to their right as they looked upstream, same side as the lodge. The grass was long and almost the color of the trout's back. What Jack thought. The bank was not high here and the brush and trees had been cleared away so that he could see the log ranch house across the field. Line of sight. Kreutzer. If he really did have a spotting scope, or a good scope on a rifle, he could probably see the silver of her earrings. What a crazy fucker, he didn't really shoot at people, did he?

Just then the fish caught her second wind, if she'd ever lost the first. Jack had begun to think of her as female, because to fight this hard she must have been full of roe and protecting her eggs. The riffle was not long and the trout lunged up it and swam into the quiet pool at the top, right at the edge of the meadow. Then, with what must have been the last shreds of her strength, she fought the pull and went deep and stopped. Unbelievable. Few humans had this much heart. Jack could not have measured his admiration. He loved the fish right then as much as anything in his world.

Alison K slowed and trotted past the wooden marker that said KEEP OUT! PRIVATE! DON'T GET SHOT! She went past it along the bank until she was level with the plunging line and he could see her breathing hard and she finally looked back. And he did not have time to tell her to please not go past the post. "Hey!" he yelled. She waved. "Hey!" He ran. He stumbled on a root, caught himself, and ran to her side; he did not slip the long net from his belt as he went.

"Hey we—we can't—" He was going to tell her that they were trespassing, that they better break off and turn back. But. He followed the taut yellow line from the bent rod straight down into the dark pool. The strength, the desperate effort it was still taking the fish to hold that depth. Fuck that. That fish, any fish, deserved better than if they parted the tippet and she swam away with a hook in her jaw and three feet of trailing line that would eventually tangle on some root and kill her. Nope, they would bring her up and release her.

"Good" was all he said. "That was really good. She is a special fish. Damn."

"Damn."

"Wanna bring her up?"

"Yes."

She did. And as she brought up the fish Jack was aware of his back in a new way, that it faced the house two hundred yards off, that the light pack he wore would not stop a thing, and though he did not believe that anyone on this river would really shoot at anyone else, he realized that he was bracing for the crack of a warning shot, the jump of a stone on the far bank.

•

She was probably three pounds. Alison K didn't care about a picture, all she wanted was to slip the tiny hook from the trout's lip and cradle her in her loosely cupped hands. Hold her against the slow current as the great fish's gills worked and her tail wavered slowly as she breathed and recovered. Alison squatted in the shallow water at the edge of the pool and held her for as long as it took. After maybe ten minutes, Jack said, "You're good? I'm gonna go see a farmer about a horse."

He really had to pee. He looked around. At the top of the pool was a ford of shallow stones and he waded across into a dense grove of spruce. He crunched onto the bed of needles and cones and unclipped the waist pack and the webbing belt and pushed down the waders. He couldn't do it fast enough. It had been a while since lunch, where he'd drunk too much iced tea, and the chase was high adrenaline and he was nearly in pain. He exhaled and was about to close his eyes and release when he noticed the strap sticking from the ground.

It was a dun green Velcro fastener. Barely emerged from disturbed duff.

It was all disturbed. A patch like the outline of a small tent. The spruce needles were darker where they had been roughed and tossed and he could see that the Velcro was the strap of a wading boot. He let go and pissed—that wave of relief—but he wasn't following the arc of the stream: in the dim light he was trying to make out the edge of the boot and then the shot cracked and a chip of bark flew from a tree five feet away.

He dropped to his knees. Mid-piss and the flow clamped. He pulled up his waders, ran his palm over the ground behind him, and found his webbing belt and clipped it, picked up the waist pack, and crouched and ran. *What the hell?*

Jack came out of the trees at a full sprint. She was standing, holding her rod in the sunlight, startled, blinking. His net was on the rocks. He splashed across the stone ford and yelled, "Downstream! Run downstream!" She was confused. She looked across the meadow, then at the river. "Go!" he yelled. "Run!" Half nod and she was moving.

CHAPTER FOUR

"I should fire you right now. If it wasn't goddamn impossible to get a decent guide mid-season, I would."

That was Kurt, who was waiting for Jack on the porch of his cabin. Kurt did not want to dress down his guide by the lodge or in the sandy track by Jack's truck where guests might see. He had dealt with one crazy client already. Alison K had been beyond pissed. She wanted to drive up to Kreutzer's right now, with Kurt, and give the sonofabitch a double-barreled reprimand. Wanted to break his damn rifle against the wall of his fancy log mansion. Kurt stood in front of her and tried to calm her, held his big hands out in air as if he were pressing down on the back of a bucking pony.

"Well, I know, I know, but we can't go over there. Gate's locked, first off, and he will never open it. Won't answer his phone, either. I know—I been through this before. Yes, the old coot should be locked up. No, the sheriff won't touch it, long as it's a warning shot. Law's unclear is why—he kinda has a right to warn folks off his property. Yes, even with a gunshot. I know. How old? Christ the bastard must be eighty if a day. Or eighty-five. Eighty-five going on fourteen if you ask me. Crazier than a loon, apparently. Yes, but he's been like that his whole life. I know."

"*Warning* shot?" Alison steamed. "Eighty-five, for chrissakes. How bad does he shake? He could've killed Jack. Or me. Jack said he hit a tree a few feet away, warning shot my ass."

She was apeshit. Jack had to hand it to Kurt: he held out those big palms and let her buck out. Never once cast blame or aspersion in her direction. Never once said, "You know, the boundary is clearly marked and it does say, 'Don't get shot!'" He never once shook his head and led with a "Just sayin'." Nope, he agreed with her one hundred percent and let her vent out her anger.

It was Jack he had words for. On the cabin porch with the stone smell of the river coming up from below.

Kurt said, "You saw the sign. Fact, I don't give a shit if you saw it, or if your eyesight is twenty–a thousand and you can't read those big block letters—I *told* you. I expressly warned you: Do-not-under-any-circumstances-go-past-the-post. I told you this was no bullshit, we had a guest shot at last year. Cody, too, and he swears he was this side of the post. But unh unh. Rules don't apply to you, maybe, and you went ahead and endangered your client, yourself, and frankly this whole operation. If word gets out—which it will—that another guest was shot at we could lose I don't even wanna guess how much potential business. God*damn*. First goddamn day."

He was not playacting. He stood beside Jack at the edge of the porch, arms crossed, looking down at the bending river silvering in the long sun coming up the canyon and he spat. A jet of chew. His jaw set tight again, chin out. As if he couldn't even bear to look at this worthless employee.

Jack opened his mouth. "I—"

Kurt held up a hand. Don't wanna hear it. Shut the fuck up. Then he reconsidered, spat. "Were you gonna apologize, sans excuses numbers one, two, and three?"

"No."

Now the manger turned with a creak of his boots on the planks. He had a lethal gleam in his eye. *"No?"*

"No. She followed the fish ten feet past the line. She fought it all the way up the riffle and it dove deep in that pool. Anybody watching could see it clear as day—that all she wanted to do was bring it up and turn around."

Kurt slipped a finger into his snap-shirt breast pocket and fished out a can of Copenhagen. He refreshed his dip and slid it back. Didn't say a word. Spat off the porch. Turned back to study the river. "Why are you here?" he said finally.

"Need work."

"Yeah?"

Kurt didn't complete the thought. He didn't have to say, "You're a stone-cold liar." They both let the question or challenge drift off the porch like a moth on the breeze. *Yeah?* But he wasn't done. Kurt said, "Guy with an education like yours, who takes up guiding, he's usually running."

Jack didn't rise. Was he running? He had no idea. He knew that when he was at home on the ranch helping his father it wasn't great to have a ton of unstructured time. It was harder these days to crack a book or take out his fishing gear. Running or not running, it was his concern, nobody else's. He was here, on contract, for the rest of the season. He was not a felon. That's about all that should matter to the lodge.

Kurt grimaced at the river, stretched his neck, rubbed his chin. "I been canoeing once or twice," he said.

Jack took a half step back as if pushed. If Kurt heard it he didn't bother to look. "Shit can happen on a river. The strangest shit. Dangerous, too. Outta nowhere. Am I right?"

If Jack had words they were stuck like pieces of ice swallowed sideways.

"I think that's why I like fishing, guiding. Pleasant mostly, but—" Kurt spat. "Shit can get crosswise so fast. Keeps you on your toes. And you don't wanna be distracted, dwelling on what all you might have done, or some fat screw-up where somebody died. I mean . . ." His head swiveled and he winced at Jack, who was staring. Kurt chuckled. "Don't look shocked. Ever Google your name? Once you screen out the real estate agent in Indiana you get a lot about a kid who was on a river expedition up by Hudson Bay that didn't turn out so well for his best friend. Three years ago, right? I'm sorry, I truly am."

Kurt tugged his hat brim down tight on his forehead, turned on his boot heel, and walked right past Jack and off the porch. He smelled of woodsmoke and burnt plastic and kerosene. "Oh," he said as he passed. "Park your truck with the others by the gate. And don't forget to bring up that thirty-thirty and whatever other guns. Bad enough that Kreutzer's shooting at folks."

•

Jack skipped dinner. He wasn't in the mood. He'd been shot at by his neighbor and dressed down by his boss all in one afternoon, and ordered to give up his Winchester lever-action .30-.30 carbine. Which he was loath to do, on principle. It gave him, if anything, moral support. Last night, after he had fetched it from the truck and leaned it in the corner, he had slept better. Also, he'd seen something that afternoon that had disturbed him: the green strap emerging from the duff of spruce needles like the nose of some small animal seeking air. And beside it, the edge of what had to be a wading boot. What was that? Where they dumped worn-out gear? But it wasn't just the shoe, it was the roughed-up ground around it, and the shape of it.

He would meet Alison K in the morning and they would fish again, maybe work on her nymphing, but tonight he wanted to stick to himself. He especially did not want to meet Kurt for fear of what he, Jack, might say or do. The man had impugned his integrity as a guide—the client's safety is always the first priority—and had basically called him a screw-up. For this day and for his past. Did he need the job this badly? No. Did he want to stay? Probably not. Did he want to get in his truck and drive out tonight? Not really. He really needed to get away from the family ranch for a while. The routine there was so ingrained, he and his father so habituated to each other, that being there was almost like standing still. Or drifting on a very slow current, and it left him altogether too much time to think and to feel. This, the fishing part, the guiding and teaching with a good client, he loved. If he could stay out of Kurt's hair, keep from tangling, he might be okay. It was good money and he could fish until November and have a small stake to take him to the next thing, whatever that might be.

He had food in the truck—packets of noodle soup and freeze-dried stroganoff that he always kept with him, and a case of Dinty Moore beef stew, in cans. Because one never knew. He also had his backpacking gear, but he wouldn't need the stove tonight as the cabin had the two burners. He'd make a modest meal—poor compared to what would be served a few hundred yards downhill—and he'd eat it on the porch and enjoy it more. Kurt hadn't said anything about being required to eat in the lodge.

Before he heated dinner, would he walk up to the office house by the gate and hand in his rifle? No. He wanted it tonight. He'd make Kurt ask him again or fire him. He'd say it slipped his mind.

He took a hot shower and heated up a can of stew. He was just buttoning his shirt when he heard footsteps on the porch and a hesitant knock on the door. He opened it. A short woman wearing a blue windbreaker with the lodge's leaping trout logo held out three folded towels. She had long black hair in a braid on her shoulder and her eyes flicked up to his and down to the towels.

"Ana?" She nodded.

"Hello. Mr. Jack?" she said.

"Yes."

"I thought you might want extra towels before I go home."

"Oh." He reached out to take them. "Thank you."

"I'm sorry about the gun."

"That's all right."

"They are very strict here."

"I'm getting that."

"If I don't report what I am supposed to report I lose my job."

"Sure."

She wouldn't look at him. Jack said, *"¿De dónde es?"*

Her head came up.

"¿De qué estado?"

"Durango."

"Lo conozco."

Her eyes widened. *"¿Sí?"*

Jack smiled. "I once bought a horse from there. From Santa Clara. There is a breeder there, famous for his cutting horses. *Fui para recogerla."*

She returned the smile, hesitant. Sad.

"Beautiful, big country. You must miss it," he said.

She nodded. "I do. *Claro.* I better get home," she said. "My little one starts first grade in a week and she—"

"She wants her mother all the time," Jack said.

"*Sí, eso es.* Okay, *buenas noches.*"

"*Á usted.*" He held up the towels. "*Gracias.*"

At the edge of the porch she turned. Something like fear crossed her face, followed by something like decision. It reminded Jack of the shadow of two hawks fighting in mid-air. She hesitated and then she said, "*Tres, tres, nueve, tres.*"

"What?" Jack said, confused.

"*Recuerde . . . Dígamelo.* Please."

"Three, three, nine, three."

She nodded and went up the path. He took the towels in and lifted the pot of stew off the burner. What the heck was that? The last part? He had no idea. He took the stew out to one of the rockers and ate straight from the stainless backpacking pot, and had the sifting of the river and the reedy peeps of flycatchers for company. He saw an osprey glide downstream into the low sun that flooded the bend with warm light. And he let the stresses of the day wash through him. He was glad to meet

Ana; she somehow took the sting out of Kurt's anger. He didn't want to think about any of it, just feel those last sprays of sun on the side of his face and eat his dinner. But he did think. He thought about Alison K, for one.

She was really famous, he was certain. A singer—he knew as soon as he heard her hum. Her voice was beautiful, even barely above a whisper. Soulful. Iconic, one of the great ones. He had heard the voice and seen her face in photos, he was certain, but couldn't place her because he was pretty much musically illiterate. He listened to the radio in his truck but that was about it. He had spent so much time in the saddle and on the creek, and reading, that he had missed the waves of musical fashion that had rocked his peers. If he had a cell signal now—which he didn't—he could search her, but he probably wouldn't anyway, out of a natural tact. To prevent the kind of intrusion he had just felt from his boss.

She was a celebrity here for some peace, for escape probably from relentless recognition, for fishing. But she did not act how Jack thought celebrities acted. She was not shuttered behind big sunglasses, she was not elusive or snotty, she seemed truly down-to-earth. More than that, he thought she had a certain bravery he rarely encountered and couldn't define; it was something to do with a willingness to look beyond the surface of things, into their heart, and he wondered if that was an essential part of being an artist. It was more than just curiosity, it seemed to him she was restless for truth somehow. How he had understood that in one day of fishing he wasn't sure, but it intrigued him. He remembered, or relived, the scent of her, leaning in against his shoulder as he showed her how to tie on a fly with an Orvis knot rather than the classic clinch knot. A blossom smell of shampoo and something almost woody, or smoky, coming off her neck, her arms. The way she had stood after lunch, straight, with her hands near her sides, and looked right into him and said yes to everything. Her lack of fear—of criticism, or of whatever they were going to try next. Her sudden surprised laugh. How she broke the tension with her candor: "It's okay. You're a boy and I'm a girl."

He would not fall in love, that was something he no way would do on the first day of a new job. He was trying to work his way into some stability, some solace maybe, not out of it. And he would not lose his heart in a mountain canyon a thousand miles from wherever this person lived. A person who probably had a million suitors, including famous musicians and actors. Millionaire producers. Who was he? A boy who had barely graduated from college because he was so stricken with the aggregated losses of his mother and his best friend. Whose past life was slipping out under his feet and who had no notion of how to approach the future. Except to try to keep this job for the next two and a half months, a prospect that seemed less certain this evening than it had been in the morning. God.

Still he could not stop seeing her fishing, the grace of her movements as she stepped across two stones, the curve and swing of her hips. Her smile, blinking into the sun; the smooth line of her jaw where it met her throat; her long neck. Husky laugh. And the way a melody carried on her voice, even when she hummed; he had never heard anything like it. Jesus. Was she flirting with him? Yes. Was she toying with him? He didn't know. She did not seem cruel in any way, or self-aggrandizing, or in need of any affirmation from anyone. She had a self-sufficiency that rivaled his father's, without the terseness. She seemed to act honestly on how she saw things and how she felt. Seemed. He was not really in any shape to judge anyone's character, was he?

Whew.

The sun dropped below the last ridge of pines downcanyon, and drew after it a train of shadow and immediate chill. Jack pushed up and out of the chair and stepped into the cabin and clapped the screen door behind him. He pulled on the thick wool fisherman's sweater that had been his grandfather's. He rinsed the pot and threw the greasy wash off the porch, then heated water for tea. He went back to the truck and found a plastic honey bear and stirred some in and returned to his creaking seat. He sipped the tea as darkness thickened.

Small bats appeared over the river, just fluttering shadows that seemed to condense out of the cool grainy air. They were soft like the air, and they flitted with a silence that belied their speed. If he listened hard he could hear now and then the slightest peep. He tried to follow one after another in aerobatic flight and lost them to the dusk and to their elaborate weavings. He envied them in a way: the simplicity of the night's errand—to catch bugs; to return to an overhang somewhere, in cliff or outbuilding. To mate, to nest. What Cheryl had wanted, with him, and right now it didn't seem at all soul killing or dull. If he could guide, just fish, and come back to this every evening, he'd be fine. More than fine. If he could keep from getting crosswise with Kurt—more crosswise—and if some new crazy virus didn't burn through the town and up the canyon.

It'd be nice to have one summer of peace.

He took the empty tea mug inside and rinsed it in the sink. He set his alarm for 5:30, though he knew he wouldn't need it, and fell asleep hard.

•

He woke suddenly to the sound of footsteps. He thought they were steps. A slow but rhythmic crunching of pine needles. Was it? There would be deer moving up and down the canyon, elk, too. Coyotes. Bear. Mountain lion for sure. Were the steps four-legged or two-? By the time he knew he was not dreaming but fully awake and his head was clear he was not sure what he'd heard. He thought in a flash it might be Alison K paying a visit. Her cabin was only a hundred and fifty yards down the bank and she seemed to know where he slept. His heart hammered and he listened hard. He wasn't sure if he wished that it was her and he sat up. But it wasn't. The creshing stopped as soon as he gave it his full attention.

Still, he swung his feet to the floor and reached for the gun. Must have been late. Through the upstream window, between the lace curtains, a nearly half-moon the color of bone struggled off the ridge. The light it cast was sallow, as if fevered, as if pushing through haze, and he thought maybe there was a fire off to the east somewhere, though he smelled no smoke.

He levered the action of the gun halfway and slid a finger into the breach and felt the brass of the round chambered there. Good. He lay the rifle across the quilt and dressed quickly. He felt for his cap on a nail by the door and had the thought as he did that Ken the Hen, the previous guide, must have hammered it there for just that purpose; the lodge would have used a fancy hand-wrought hook. This had been Ken's cabin. And then the image of the wading boot barely seen in the spruce grove sent goose bumps up his arms.

Murder? No way. But then he hadn't thought it possible that a neighbor would shoot at him, either.

If someone was casing his cabin he wanted to know. He picked up the rifle and he pushed out through the screen, yawing the spring, and closed it gently behind him. Very carefully, he stepped over the boards and off the upstream side of the porch. The moon threw a feeble light over the canyon but he moved into the shadows of the dense trees and he found a large ponderosa among the lodgepole and leaned against it. As he would if he were waiting for an approaching elk. The smell off the bark he loved, like strong vanilla. He listened. A still night with the breeze stirring downstream, following the river. He could hear the muffled rush of it, of the rapid above the bridge where she had run with her valiant fish. Whatever had been moving was stopped and waiting or gone. He flared his nostrils. He knew deer smell and bear and the musk of bull elk in rut, which would be beginning now. A person's deodorant could give them away. Nothing.

What the hell. He didn't have a whole lot to lose, he was on the verge of getting fired anyway. He really needed to know.

He slung the rifle and walked quietly across the slope to the trail that descended to the river. If someone stopped him, which they wouldn't, he would say he was going night fishing, one of his favorite pastimes. If they asked him why he didn't have a rod, he'd say he'd leaned it against a tree back a ways while he scouted. Fuck 'em.

He went down the steep path, and turned upstream when he hit the river and the fishermen's trail, and crossed the bridge. On the other side he followed it easily by moonlight to where it ended abruptly in a pile of boulders fifty yards below Kreutzer's line. He could see, across the river and upstream, the opening of the meadow and the dreaded post.

He climbed over the rocks. He threaded in and out of willow brush, at the edge of the wall of trees. He could see the moon clearly floating in the ragged V of the canyon. It was dirty, almost spectral, its light wan, but he felt exposed and wished it had been two hours earlier when the night was only stars and much darker.

When he got to the grove of black timber he was glad for the richer darkness. He pushed into the spruce and prickled his cheeks on the sharp needles. When he reached the small opening in the middle where he thought he had peed, he peered out and could see the lights of Kreutzer's lodge. The night was very still. The long pool where Alison had netted her fish quieted the creek and he could hear crickets in the grass on the opposite bank.

He knelt and ran his hands over the duff of needles where he thought the boot might be but felt nothing. He had a headlamp in his fishing waist pack but he was loath to use it. He crawled forward and made another semicircle with his palms. He closed his eyes to focus better and then he heard it. A thrum, very faint, he thought it sounded like a motor, and then a heavy door, not slammed but solidly closed, and then a shriek.

Was it a barn owl? They sound some nights like a woman being murdered. This one rose to a terrible pitch like the owl's but was silvery and sharp and thin. And then it clipped short.

Silence.

Even the crickets had ceased. No motor now, no door, nothing.

It took him a second to sit up, to move his limbs again. To hear anything but the thudding of his heart. Nothing again, same as before. He dug the headlamp out of his waist pack and took off his cap and shielded the lamp on the river side and thumbed the switch over to the red beam. Red light did not affect night vision and it would be harder to see from Kreutzer's.

He scanned the ground and scanned it again. And felt his heart begin to race. This was where he had stood for sure. But the ground that had been rough with disturbed needles was now smooth and dry as if combed. Haphazard spruce cones lay where he had seen the boot. Maybe he was wrong, maybe he was ten feet off. He risked it. He brought the red light up along the trunk he remembered and there was the pale scar of the shot that had missed him, a patch of missing bark and splintered cambium. Here. Here had been a boot, for sure. No longer.

He was not going around the bend. He had seen it. It was not a fiction-reader's imagination. Strap, Velcro, edge of wading boot. He fitted the elastic headband of the light to his head and knelt on all fours and began digging with his hands.

CHAPTER FIVE

Daybreak. Gray light moved among the trunks of the pines.

Before he had turned back downstream he had dug away the duff in a ten-foot circle. All he found was a nipper for cutting line—a modified toenail clipper with a rainbow trout enameled on the back. It could have belonged to any fisherman.

But he could not shake the scream.

He had hiked back to the cabin, undressed, and laid the rifle beside him. His thoughts had spun but after a while exhaustion overtook him and he finally slept. He dreamt of the Encampment, the three of them and the four horses stringing along the high trail, the roar of the gorge below and the slick tilt of the slab rock that his father was about to ride over. But this time his mother reined up and turned in the saddle and faced him, her eyes severe above a strange half smile, and she said, "You ride first today."

It should have been a good dream but it wasn't. It should have meant that her life would be spared. That he, on his stolid gelding Duke, would walk just fine across the slick angle of rock and she would follow. But he woke with a cry in his throat and his heart racing. Jesus. He needed to settle down. He needed to take stock and figure out where he was, who he was. He lay on the bed and looked out between the tied-back curtains and breathed. After Wynn had died he had suffered nightmares often, and wakings like this that felt less like release than a panic attack. One symptom. He had read about PTSD and all of this was classic. And survivor's guilt. Even paranoia. Even imaginings—a softer word than *hallucinations*, which was softer still than *psychosis*. But tonight he was not imagining or hallucinating or psychotic, he was sure. He had seen what he had seen and heard what he had heard.

•

He watched the first light quicken the trees and then he roused and splashed himself with cold water. Then he did something that surprised him. He took the .30-.30 out into the pines and leaned it against the upstream side of one of the trunks. It could only be seen from a patch of woods no one would ever walk. If Kurt asked him about it he'd say he'd gotten rid of it. He hadn't been fired yesterday, what was one more strike?

He found himself forgoing his own quiet cup of coffee here on his porch, found himself wanting to see Alison K. Somehow the thought of her by the hearth with her first cup was reassuring. He hoped she was there and walked down.

She was there. So was Mr. Silver Buttons and his partner, Neave. Alison K was standing by the fire, the couple were in a leather love seat, their cups on an exquisite coffee table made from a slab of petrified wood.

The man—what was his name?—smiled at Jack wanly. Jack did a double take. Mr. Silver Buttons did not have the quietly arrogant assurance of the possible hedge-fund billionaire Jack had met two nights before. He was different. He looked debauched somehow, his eyes shiny and too big but also veiled. He seemed ashamed maybe, like someone who had spent the night bingeing on something. Was he sick? Jack noticed a Band-Aid on the back of his left hand. She just looked exhausted, if not drugged. Her long black hair was pinned up and her smile was sincere and tired, but her eyes were hooded as if she were half-asleep. She wore a shirt with thumb loops that pulled the sleeves down to the first knuckles of her hand. To hide maybe a Band-Aid or puncture.

Jack nodded good morning and fetched his own cup. Someone with a sense of fun or kitsch had put out mugs with animal graphics. He chose a bull elk stepping out of golden aspen and bugling, his breath steaming in the autumn chill. Jack hesitated between pulling the spigot on Kona dark roast or Sumatran blond and chose the dark. He stirred in a teaspoon of honey. Then he was curious about which mugs the rich couple had chosen and as he joined Alison at the fire he raised his cup, *Cheers,* and the guests raised theirs: Silver Buttons lifted a wolf, his wife a mountain goat. Alison touched her cutthroat to his elk.

Her smile: what he had hungered for since his head had hit the pillow six hours ago. Since he had gotten back to the cabin safely and turned the dead bolt in the door and lain down. Safely? Had he been unsafe? He didn't know. He didn't really know a thing and every day it seemed he knew less. And he'd only been here two days.

She smiled and sipped from the trout cup and her eyes were steady over the rim. "You okay?" she said.

Over his own cup he blinked fast twice. He hadn't meant to.

"Not really?" she said.

They were on the other side of the wide stone fireplace from the love seat and the fire was popping and shirring but still he glanced at the couple and kept his voice low. "Not sure," he said.

"Didn't sleep well?"

"No."

"Me neither."

"No?"

"I heard an owl. One of those screamers."

Jack shivered. Didn't mean to do that, either. Cardinal rule in guiding: Don't scare easy. If you do scare, absolutely DO NOT LET THE CLIENT KNOW. Your job—one of many—is to keep your cool. Resolve the situation, mitigate the danger, go on with your day. And keep the client blissfully unaware of all of it if possible. Kind of a river guide's creed. Probably a climber's, too, and a platoon leader's, maybe a parent's.

"A barn owl," he got out.

"Yes, that's the one. Sounds like a woman being knifed to death. We had them at home."

"What I always thought, too. Sounds grisly." He wondered if she'd heard the same shriek, and how. No way she could have heard it from her cabin. "Window open?" he said.

She shook her head. "No. I was walking." She sipped. His shock: if he'd been trying to hide his emotions, he wasn't doing a very good job. She laughed. "You look gobsmacked."

"I do?"

"Can't a girl walk the hills at night?"

"Yeah, sure." He steadied himself. "Like in 'The Long Black Veil.'"

"Ooh, yeah. I was thinking more like 'Walkin' After Midnight.'"

"Patsy Cline."

"You're good."

And she started to sing it, softly, just over the flutter and sighs of the fire. Despite herself. Jack might have stared. Her voice was as sweet and rough-grained and passionate as any he had heard in his life. Last night he'd been rooted to the earth by a shriek. Now it was song. "I stopped to see a weeping willow / Cryin' on his pillow . . ." He knew the voice now, too. Holy crap. She had lifted her chin and turned her head and her eyes had closed, as if singing to the sky beyond the pitched roof of the lodge, or to a memory, and she opened them for a sec and caught his look, and the phrasing stopped midair. Just—Jack thought—as the scream had. "Sorry," she said.

"Fuckin' A," Jack mouthed.

"Now you know."

"Never be sorry."

"Why, thanks."

"Where were you walking?"

The bell chimed and they all turned and saw Shay rapping the clapper cord. She wore a deep purple blouse the color of a midnight sky.

•

"Where were you walking?" Jack asked again after Shay had poured them coffee.

"Upstream."

"To the bridge?"

"Over it. And up." She spread marmalade over a homemade sourdough English muffin. Jack was beginning to see last night's foray as from owl view, or drone. At one point, they must have been very close.

"You walked over the bridge?"

She nodded and kept her attention on the second half of the muffin, blueberry jam this time. The camera would have recorded both of them for sure.

"Um, mind if I ask?"

"You mean what the heck was I doing up there in the middle of the night?"

"Just wondering."

"Bird-watching."

"Bird-watching. You had binocs?"

"Yep. I did it my first night, too. One of my hobbies, but that night I went for a walk upstream and I was looking and listening for real birds."

"Goddamn."

"Excuse me?"

"Kreutzer's an old bird. A crazy old coot. Is that it?"

"Yep."

"He shot at you, or me, and you were pissed, and you wanted to see what the heck. Bird-watching."

"Polite way of putting it. He shot at my favorite guide." She lifted the marmaladed muffin, took a bite, let her hazel eyes settle on his. Jack thought that they were the color of stones on the riverbed.

"Did you see anything?"

"The windows were lit but there was no movement." What he had seen. She said, "I heard an owl scream. One time. Owls usually repeat."

"Yeah," Jack said. "Usually."

"I thought I heard a car."

He wondered then if she had lain awake as he had, her head spinning with questions.

"You wanna start downstream this morning?" Jack said. "We can start at the fence and work up. Those two ledge drops are fun."

"Okay."

"I'm kind of sick of the bridge."

"Me, too."

•

They ate. Eggs Benedict with smoked trout. Dollar pancakes with whipped butter and real maple syrup. Two quarts of coffee, at least. *What could be better?* Jack's mantra. *What could be better than this?* Nothing, if you focused on the breakfast, the company, the fishing they were about to do.

The early morning hadn't been as cold and there had been no frost, and now the breeze huffed intermittently upstream, which was less normal in the morning, and it brought with it a breath of warmth and fleets of flat-bottomed clouds. Whatever rust Alison K had accumulated over a summer of touring she had now shed, and she worked the river with confidence and fewer and fewer comments from Jack. He was enjoying just watching her. He helped her with fly selection and performed the always-appreciated guide's service of tying on, but then he stepped back. She caught fish and he netted them and she held and released them. She said it was important for her to touch them, help them recover.

Jack loved mornings like this. The clouds sailed together and multiplied, so that by late morning the sky was a running scud of overcast. The air over the river seemed relieved of relentless sun and released a wealth of summer smells—the damp of exposed roots, the faint sweetness of black-eyed Susans, a watery scent of crushed horsetails. And rain. The promise of it. As they waded above the second ledge and entered the bend below the lodge it did begin to shower. It was nearly lunchtime anyway, so they decided to trot up the trail to the lodge. She had caught so many fish, and she thought it might be a nice afternoon for a sauna and a massage, and she asked Jack if, after lunch, they might reconvene for a late-afternoon session.

•

He hadn't noticed the awning before. It rolled out from a red-wood casing under the eaves and covered two-thirds of the back deck and the rain ran off it.

Lunch today was more communal. In the shelter of the awning, which ticked and pattered. Jack smelled the spread before they had gone up the steps—a briny scent of ocean—and it evoked a sharp memory of coastal Maine, the paddling trips he and Wynn had taken to the Penobscot and the islands. Two long tables were laid with a bounty of seafood: warm lobster tails beside a boat of drawn butter, shucked oysters on ice, yellowtail sashimi, a bowl of ikura with lemons and another of beluga caviar. And because it was raining and the day was cooling: fresh clam chowder, hot. And three species of green salad and a grandma's potato salad, and a chicken salad in case a guest wasn't feeling maritime.

Shay glided out with a tray of warm salmon toast and she was wearing a sailor shirt and a Royal Navy cap cocked on her head. Whoa. Jack never thought the lodge would stoop that low. He thought of Uncle Lloyd talking about the Caribbean cruise he'd won at the Cattlemen's Association banquet. When he got back, he and Jack were irrigating the narrow hayfields across the river and Jack had asked him how it was. Lloyd stepped into the shade of a cottonwood and leaned on his double-aught spade. He said,

"I didn't have enough shirts."

"Shirts?" Jack said.

"Well, first there was Hawaiian Night. I had a Hawaiian shirt so I wore that. Lucky damn thing. Then there was French Night.

Were we anchored off of Haiti? Who the hell knows. I wore the Hawaiian shirt. Got some looks. Then there was Las Vegas Night. I mean. One genius who must've actually read the packing list wore a sky blue tuxedo."

"You wore the Hawaiian shirt."

"Yep."

"Fuckin' A."

"What I said."

Jack figured that the types who patronized the lodge wouldn't tolerate forced festivity, but he guessed this was more a themed meal. Well, Shay was cute in her outfit and at least the guests didn't have to share a communal table.

The mood was a bit festive, he had to admit. The fleecy couple were there, as were Will and Neave, and the general energy was much improved. The two couples stood and conversed together, and a peal of laughter rang over the river. They turned and motioned Alison over and Jack stepped away to give her some space. Shay circulated with a tray of iced teas and bull shots—beef bouillon and vodka, with lemon—when the rain swept over the awning with a final rush, and ceased. Shay set down the tray and rolled back the awning.

"We'll give this a try," she announced.

The sky did lighten. Still a mass of moving clouds, but no longer low enough to scrape the rim of the canyon. Shay rang a handbell and everyone lined up. Jack was at the end of the line with Cody when they heard a faint drum and then the shuddering thwop of a chopper and all eyes turned skyward and the belly of a black Robinson helicopter sheared right over the trees downstream, heading up the canyon. It passed over, the shadow of a giant bird, and seemed to be descending. As fast as it had appeared, it was gone, the beat of the rotors fading in a trail of Dopplered low notes. But the thrum did not quite cease.

It had landed. That's what Jack thought. Just upstream. He held his plate with the single lobster tail and turned to Cody. Who wore a half grin.

"The king has arrived," Cody said.

"The king?"

"Den."

"But I thought—"

"You thought he was in London or wherever. Yesterday. He probably was."

That's not what Jack was thinking. He was thinking that it sounded like the chopper had landed at Kreutzer's, and he'd been told that the place belonged to an adversarial neighbor—

He shut his mouth. Cody said, "The dude has like twenty properties all over the world. Can't say 'houses,' cuz some are like frigging towns. I hear he's got a fishing lodge in Kamchatka makes this place look ghetto."

"Kamchatka?"

Cody had the half grin but his eyes were flat, as they always were. "He invites special guests from everywhere. Supposed to be the best trout fishing on earth."

Did Jack hear a note of wistfulness? Maybe. He took two oysters, skipped the yellowtail, which he knew was just about extinct, and spooned a heap of chicken salad.

•

They didn't talk much over lunch. They sat at their table by the railing. Alison told him the helicopter was Den, and Jack said he'd heard, and their eyes met for a thoughtful beat and they let it go. For now. After that they ate. They had shared an easy, quiet closeness all morning in the river and both intuited that the best conversation now was silence. At some point, in the midst of it, Jack thought he heard the rising cadence of the chopper's engines, but this time they saw no bird.

They skipped dessert. She was eager for a massage and a rest and they decided they'd convene around three to fish.

•

The rain fell again, softly, by the time he walked the road to his cabin. Almost his favorite kind of afternoon: intermittent squalls and drizzle so fine it was scarcely denser than fog. But today he barely noticed. When he got to his shack Jack changed fast into quick-dry hiking pants and zipped into an olive rain jacket. He dug eight-power binocs out of his fishing pack and slung them under the jacket and stuffed his lightweight hiking boots into a CamelBak and went out the door. He tugged his wet waders and wading boots on again and picked up his rod as before and trotted down the trail to the river.

•

Between the lodge and his cabin the river made a shallow S-turn and in the middle of it was a stretch of water that could not be seen except by someone fishing, or hiking, into it. He crossed where the river was shallowest. He held up the rod and acted like a man on a mission to fish, finally free of clients and with only God as witness. He turned up the game trail as if angling to fish the top of the bend and he disappeared into the shadows of some big ponderosas and as soon as he was out of sight he set the rod down against a trunk. It was also good to be alone. Alone alone. It occurred to him then that he had not seen Cody or the fleecy young couple on the river all morning. Again. Curious. Where had they worked up such a hunger for lunch?

The rain had lightened to a near mist. He pried off the wading boots, slid off the waders, twisted the hiking boots out of the pack, and put them on. Then he climbed away from the river and up the rocky side of the canyon, trying to stay in the lodgepoles.

•

He wanted, as much as anything, to study the country. It always took a living look to understand how a piece of country tied together—how the ridges ran, and the drainages, and the peaks.

But what he really wanted was to get a bird's-eye view of the lodge; and of Kreutzer's.

He found a game trail as he always did, and the north side of the canyon steepened fast. Soon he was climbing on a trace gritted with loose gravel and using his hands now and then to climb through the ledges of sandstone. He crossed pocket benches of wheatgrass and saw the scat of hare and deer, and the twisted links of a small predator, probably bobcat. None of the sign was very new, which made sense: in a summer this bountiful with rain most of the animals were up high.

He climbed. He skirted a tower of sandstone jutting from the pines and the trail topped out into a grove of aspen and he found himself looking through their dripping leaves to the flying scud of the sky. He left the track and brushed through thick ferns and worked himself toward the river. As he did, he heard the faint rush. He saw an opening in the trees. He crouched. A hunter's instinct. He pushed through a screen of serviceberry and then he was out in the rain on a rock ledge. He crawled. Got to the lip beside a broken slab of sandstone and he peered over.

He could see it all. He must have climbed almost eight hundred feet. The canyon was shaped like a broad funnel. Upstream, to his left, in the widest part of it, were woods and Kreutzer's wide hayfield. The river ran down the near side of the tapering funnel and the county highway down the far side. The canyon walls angled toward each other, pinched the road and the river closer together. Still plenty of room: enough to give the river its wildness. And there, right below him, were the bends they had fished, the lodge in the tightest part of the canyon. Through the trees, he could see a short ribbon of paved county highway outside the gate. He could see the massive steel gate and its cogs. The tall hurricane fence, chain-link, on either side of it running into the pines. He could see the massage and pool cabins, trout pond, a couple of guest cabins in the woods, not his. As he scanned with naked eyes he saw a figure come out of the lodge and toss a bucket over the bank and into the trees. Shay, he could see the white sailor shirt. Probably tossing bacon grease from breakfast; she didn't care about the rain. He let his eyes travel back to his left and he saw the main office house. Half a dozen cars and trucks parked in the lot. Not Kurt's black Ford. Again to the river: he could see the bridge. He followed the flurry of white above it and lost it at the bend, but found it again in the riffle below the sign on its hated post. He worked the binocs out of his rain jacket and set his elbows on the rocks and scanned.

There in the field was Kreutzer's log house. The central core with tall windows, two stories, and the lower wings, symmetrical and ranch style, on either side. In the middle was an octagonal tower, a crow's nest, also made of logs, surrounded by windows like a control tower. Like the main lodge, Kreutzer's had a wide deck on the river side of the building, but this one had planters with trained Japanese pines and a single rectangular table in the middle. Jack adjusted the focus and saw three chairs.

Next, he followed the long drive that curved from the log mansion out through the hay meadow. At the paved road, through a gap in the trees, he could see signposts. Probably as inviting as the sign on the river. But then something curious. There was a hedgerow of pines screening the meadows and lodge from the highway; many fine houses had the same. And just inside the trees, at the edge of the fields, was another massive steel gate. No cogs or engraved trout, but similar dimensions, similar state of rust, as if they'd been installed at a similar time. And a hurricane fence, same height and design, running up- and downcanyon. He followed it downstream with the binocs. The fence entered trees and appeared in gaps and he could see it running straight into the visible line of the lodge's chain-link. As if they were the same property.

Made no sense. He heard the faint rip of traffic and he lowered the binocs and saw a camper van hauling a johnboat heading down the county road, and passing it going the other way a 4Runner with kayaks and an Audi with bikes on the roof. Everybody enjoying the green late summer, not too concerned, clearly, with any virus or if it was going to cause another pandemic. Why wasn't he? Enjoying himself? He lifted the glasses. He saw movement by the highway again and this time there were four vehicles and they were turning into Kreutzer's drive: a full-size black pickup with ladder rack, followed by a white van, windowless—Jack refocused and saw a logo and the word PLUMBING—then a dull silver four-door pickup with a door sign he couldn't read. Cody? Cody had a gray Silverado, no topper, no rod rack. Jack had seen it his first afternoon, and it had a sign painted on the front doors that said CODY'S PREMIUM GUIDE SERVICE. At the rear of the line was a white squad car with a bar light and a gold badge decal on the front door.

Jack felt rain trickling into the back of his collar. He turned his head and spat and watched again as the big gate ground open and the little convoy entered and the steel plates slid closed behind them.

•

He lowered the binoculars and rubbed his eyes with the back of a hand. He felt a faint queasiness of vertigo. Kreutzer. *He's a batshit crazy old coot.* Isn't that what Kurt had said? *Can't go talk to him 'cause the gate is locked, he'd never open it.* Something like that? And his boss was burning mad at Jack for putting a client, and the business, at risk. And now. Now Kurt was driving right up to this volatile neighbor's house, right through a gate that looked exactly like the lodge's own, followed, it seemed, by Cody. Who had warned him strictly to stay to his side of the sign when fishing, who said he had gotten shot at himself. And it was looking more and more like Kreutzer was not a neighbor at all but another lodge on a contiguous section of land. Looked to Jack like the same fence, same property. And he'd bet the ranch that Den had landed there. There was no helipad but so what? He could have landed on the driveway, it was wide enough. What the heck? He scooted back and stood and let himself steady. He tucked the binoculars back into his jacket and beat tracks the way he had come.

CHAPTER SIX

Three summers ago he had gone on a river trip with his best friend. Not just any river, but one of the most remote on the continent, a big stream that flowed out of a string of lakes far from any outpost and ran over two hundred miles into Hudson Bay. It began as a late-summer idyll, a paddler's dream: fishing, blueberry picking, camping on islands with moose that had never seen a man. They had no satellite phone, had left their watches, and planned to call the flight out from the Cree village of Wapahk when they got to the bay. On their own time. But the season had other ideas. It sent them early frost, and fire, and strangers whose intentions were not at all kind; and turned their sojourn into a fierce struggle for survival, and into the kind of tragedy that the rest of a long life might not heal or prayer redeem.

If he lived that long. If he learned to pray.

After Wynn's death Jack found his solace in fishing and reading, as he had when his mother died. In work, too, alongside his father and Uncle Lloyd. And so here on this river, he might have found a haven in fishing and work together, but he didn't.

He scooted into the trees and found his way back along the beaten trace through ferns, back down the faint game trails and over rockfall, kicking loose stones as he went. He tumbled out into the stand of ponderosas and changed back into waders and boots and picked up his rod again and stepped out into the river. He casted ahead as he waded back downstream. He fished as a man fished who was not that interested in catching anything, but was late for a date and heading home and dropping his flies in as he went. In case anyone was watching. Who would be watching? His boss and his colleague Cody were busy doing other things. Other what? Hell if he knew. He wouldn't care, either, except that he was beginning to feel that he needed to.

He caught two fish, despite himself. His date, or appointment, was waiting for him in one of the chairs on the lodge porch. She set a cup of tea on a side table. The rain had stopped and her own light Gore-Tex jacket was hanging over the chair. Her strung rod was in the rack just off the porch.

"Can I put your rain jacket in my pack?" he said. "Looks like it stopped, but it'd be good to bring."

"Okay." She rocked forward and stood. "You still look funny."

"Funny?"

"Disturbed. A little."

"I went fishing," he said lamely.

"Oh?" She raised an eyebrow. "Should I be jealous?"

"Probably not."

"Didn't catch anything?"

"A couple."

"Do you want to go again?"

The question stung. That a client might ask that of her guide. It hurt his professional pride. But then he wasn't acting at all like a pro these days.

Engender enthusiasm. His first fishing boss, Jeff Streeter, was a legendary guide up in Saratoga, Wyoming, and he had said that to him on his first day. Jack was only sixteen then. Jeff had said, "You've got good technique, Jack. Really good. And a handle on a lot of deep fishing knowledge. Kind of amazing for someone your age. It's great. Pass on as much of that as your client wants to absorb. But that's not your main job. Your main job is to engender enthusiasm."

Jack, who had been shy of the world since his mother had tried to hold the scrabbling mare to the steep hillside, and failed, and slipped with the horse into air, into a flooded gorge—he didn't know if that was a job he could accomplish. Enthusiasm was not an emotion or state of being he could much relate to. He wasn't against it, he just approached the few joys in his life in a different, maybe quieter, way. Or maybe he never approached joy at all. If he ever felt anything like it, it was because the elation snuck up on him, as it had in the river here on his first afternoon. Which he guessed was two days ago but seemed much longer.

Did he want to go fishing again? "Of course," he said. "I actually enjoy watching you fish. Can't say that about many."

She smiled, maybe relieved. "Well, let's go, pardner." She handed him her jacket, pulled her rod off the rack, and went straight for the railroad-tie steps that led down to the river trail.

•

She led him this afternoon. He thought she was going to turn left at the river and go downstream to start at Ellery's fence, but she didn't. She turned up, and didn't unhook her line until she was at the fast water and big boulders below his cabin. She said she thought she might try nymphing a stone fly and a prince, what did he think?

"Awesome. Awesome idea."

She did a double take. That wasn't a word that came out of his mouth. Was he trying to be enthusiastic? He wondered himself. He definitely did not feel centered at the moment. *Jeez,* he thought, *relax.* But he couldn't stop seeing the trucks turning into Kreutzer's drive, and the van between them.

She waded to her hips behind the largest boulder, and threw a short cast into fast water. And she held her rod high and almost horizontal just like a conductor with wand about to launch a movement. Then she followed the line as it was swirled downstream, and kept it tight and nearly vertical. She was nymphing almost like a European, and Jack was surprised and truly enjoyed watching. She hummed. Jack noticed that even when she murmured a melody, sounding barely above the burbles of the water, it thrummed through her whole body like a cello. Wynn had always said that Jack hummed unconsciously all the time—when he paddled, when he sliced cheese, when he scanned with binocs—and he had never known. He wondered if she did.

Her indicator was an orange plastic bubble not much bigger than a garbanzo bean, and when it hitched, hesitated ever so slightly, she raised her right hand—not jerked, but lifted it with firm intent—and set the hook and had one on. Wow, good. Jack thrilled and he didn't say a word as she brought in a nice brown, but he unshucked the long-handled net and waded in.

She moved up and caught another from a pocket just upstream. She cradled her rod in her left arm and bent to unhook it, and this one, a heavy rainbow, squirmed and swam off without ceremony. She stood and Jack withdrew the net and they were shoulder to shoulder. Fishing was work and he could smell the heat coming off her neck, and a spicier scent, lavender maybe, probably from the massage. She looked up at him and let a strand of hair settle across her cheek. They were nearly opposite where he had crossed the river earlier. He didn't glance at the ponderosas or let himself think again about the vehicles, the opaque house. Her mouth opened, her eyes flickered, and she closed it.

"I like fishing," she said suddenly. "A lot. But what the fuck is going on around here?"

•

"Wanna sit?" he said.

"Sure."

He gestured at the near bank and they waded over. They sat on a rounded boulder. He reached down and slid a bottle of Gatorade from a side pocket of the pack.

"Thanks," she said, and unscrewed the top, drank, handed it back.

"Did you ever talk to Mr. Den?" Jack said.

"The owner? Yes. My manager arranged for me to talk to him. Den wanted to assure me."

"Assure you?"

"Yes. That they had many celebrity guests, and very well-to-do people, and that they took security very seriously."

"Rich as shit," Jack murmured.

"Hunh?"

"The silver-button guy and his young wife, Will and Neave. They are very well-to-do. Very."

"I thought so, too. 'Rich as shit' seems right."

"So are the fleecy couple," Jack said. "Just a hunch." She nodded. "So what did Mr. Den say?"

"He said that they have their own highly trained security team and that I would never have to think about it. They had never had a problem, not once."

"I haven't seen any security team," Jack said.

"Me neither."

"Did he have an accent?"

"Oh yeah. Posh. Harrow or Eton. Oxford, probably. I could tell you what county in North Carolina, but I'm not too good with the Brits."

"He watches us from the bridge," Jack said.

"What?"

"He sits up in his town house in Chelsea and watches us fish. Cody told me. And now he's here. Probably in front of a screen."

"No kidding. I noticed the camera. I thought it was so that the lodge could make sure no locals busted their private water."

"That, too."

"What else?" she said.

"What else what?"

She took the Gatorade from his hand and elbowed him in the ribs. Not softly. "Spill it. You got a canary's tail sticking out of your mouth. Have had almost since I met you. You don't know whether to cough it up or run."

He turned for the pack. "Want chocolate or lodge-cured prosciutto? Shay gave me some of both." She elbowed him again, harder.

"Ow."

"Don't mess with me. I'm old enough to be at least your older sister."

"That's a freaky North Carolina way of putting it." He handed her a bar of Lindt dark chocolate with sea salt.

"Don't make easy cracks, either," she said. "I'm serious. What else?"

The breeze was up and the scud had lightened and the sun was white and swam in it. When he looked at her he had to squint.

"Don't you wish we could just fish?" he said. "Always fish on? And not deal with . . ." He trailed off.

"No," she said. "No, I like to work. And I like to know what the fuck the oddballs and mystics and creeps are doing all around me. You wanna go to dinner?" she said.

"Dinner?"

"You, me, your truck, Crested Butte."

"Definitely. Yes." He didn't have to think for a second.

"Well, let's go. Happy hour probably ends at six."

•

She met him at his truck in the lot inside the gate. "How'd you know it was mine?" he said.

She was dressed in tight jeans and engraved cowboy boots and a short blue wool jacket, almost felt, with a wild rose embroidered up one sleeve. He thought she looked understated and gorgeous. "Doh," she said. "Rod rack and a Colorado Cattlemen's Association sticker on the rear window."

"Hold on, I'll tell them in the office we won't be here for dinner."

"Already did. Between here and my cabin, I got intercepted three times. Young people I've never seen kept asking if I needed any help. Two of them actually stammered when I told them we were going to town."

"Huh."

"Off the reservation," she said. "I swear, I'm starting to feel claustrophobic."

Jack didn't say anything. He unlocked the truck and held the passenger door. Before she got in he reached past her and picked up a discarded chew tin, an empty can of Southern Style

Sweet Tea, and two spent tippet rolls. He didn't see any trash can nearby so he tossed them onto the Xtra cab seat in back. "Sorry."

"You should see mine." She thanked him and got in and he started up, backed out, pulled up to the keypad on its post at the gate, and punched in the numbers on the tag Kurt had given him. He realized he was holding his breath for the two seconds it took for the chains and cogs to respond.

•

They drove down the canyon. The overcast was breaking up and the shadows of the pines slid up the windshield and some-times they came around a curve and the low sun was in their eyes and they winced until they were back in shadow. The air was cool and poured in the open windows. It smelled of woods after rain. In a few miles the valley widened and they could see the river flurrying through the bends, and hayfields and ranch houses set back under cottonwoods. Jack was surprised: he suddenly relaxed. He had not realized that his chest and shoulders had been tight maybe ever since Kurt had showed him his bunk. He relaxed and something opened inside him and he glanced at Alison K, who was singing out the window. He could barely hear her in the buffeting of the wind rushing past but it made him . . . something. Happy, maybe. Maybe.

They drove. At Kit's Cabin Cutoff, they crossed the river on the steel bridge and took the dirt road that climbed away from the stream through mostly open country, sage and grass with islands of black timber and aspen. The sun had broken through and it was nice to get a wide view again. A big redtail soared and circled high ahead of them. In the rearview, Jack saw a Sprinter camper van and a black Jeep Cherokee also crossing the bridge.

"I love this country," Alison said over the wind.

"Me, too."

"I like the river a lot, but it's good to get out."

They drove over a low divide of scattered juniper and aspen and down into the Gunnison valley. When they hit the bottom where fields spread along the big river, they turned upstream and drove the highway into Crested Butte. They passed the high school ballfields and a movie theater and at a two-story stone house with a brass placard by the entrance that said LIBRARY, they turned up Elk Avenue. Cute. Little miner's houses of log and slat board gussied up with neweled porches painted in lilac and turquoise. Clapboard false fronts and little flower beds. Bookstore, two fly shops, half a dozen cafés, a score of restaurants. Ice cream shop, mountain bike store, art galleries. The rock-banded ski mountain loomed over all of it.

Tourist heaven. On a mid-August late afternoon the town was packed, zero parking spots. Locals zigzagged through the crawling traffic on cruiser bikes with an air of invincibility. A few people wore face masks, but not many.

"Yikes," Alison said. But she was enjoying every second. She had put on her baseball cap and aviator shades and stuck her elbow out the window.

"They painted it blue," Jack said.

"What?"

"Bud Light painted this whole street blue. The pavement. End to end. Paid the town."

"You're kidding."

"Not kidding."

"Did they respect themselves in the morning?"

"I don't think it had a lot to do with respect."

"Wow."

They turned right on Third and drove two blocks before they found a spot in front of a swaybacked shack with Tibetan prayer flags strung over the porch and a stained-glass Tree of Life hanging in the kitchen window. Four mountain bikes leaned against a splintered porch rail.

"Thank God for hippies," Alison said.

"Hippies with portfolios," Jack said. He nodded at the cabin. "Nine hundred thousand for that shed," he said. "At least."

"Damn."

He was about to shove open his door but held off for a passing black Jeep. Two youngish men in black caps and shades, one with a light beard. Fishermen, probably.

He and Alison got out and walked back to the main drag. The sun was low over the ridges above town. They turned onto Elk Avenue and let the warmth wash against their backs. It felt good. Jack never knew he'd been chilled in a river until he got truly warm again.

"Ice cream or beer?" he said.

"Both, of course," and she took his hand. It felt friendly, and natural, and after about five seconds he didn't think about it.

•

When they were settled at a table by the front window of the Dogwood, with sweating longneck Blowdown ales and a plate of nachos between them—"Real cheese!" the young waitress had promised brightly through her surgical mask—Alison K slipped her shades off and propped them on the brim of her cap and tipped back the bottle. It was a long drink. Jack was glad she didn't make a toast. The place was packed. They'd had their temperature taken at the door, but almost none of the customers wore masks. Loud clamor of clacking dishes and classic rock, boisterous conversation. The lowlander tourists were generally fatter than the athletic locals and more warmed up and definitely having the most fun. The fishing lodge was starting to seem particularly somber.

Alison set her bottle on the table, smacked her lips, and said, "So what else?"

"I was just starting to relax," Jack said.

"Me, too. And . . . ? There's some kinda weird shit going on back at the ranch. Did you see Neave and Will this morning?"

"Are those really their names?"

"Who knows. That's how they were introduced. They looked like zombies, no joke. Like they had just feasted on flesh. He had a Band-Aid on the back of his hand."

"I saw it."

"Like from an IV. And she—who knows. Looked like she'd been hit by a truck. Covered up the back of *her* hand with her sleeve."

"Saw that, too."

"And then at lunch they were all fine. What else did you see? Not joking. That scream or owl or whatever was freaky. And that German bastard whatever-his-name-is shooting at everyone—"

"Kreutzer."

"Yeah, him. So I'm not gonna ask again."

Jack looked away from her and out the window at the sidewalk and the streaming tourists. Through a break in the cars he noticed across the street a little girl trotting down the steps of Sheep Dog Creamery ahead of her parents and she waved her cone and dumped it on the sidewalk. Her face crumpled and her mom rushed in and Jack glanced away but his attention snagged on a man next to the doorway, turned in profile and leaning against a post; he had a blond beard and black cap and T-shirt and he was eating a cone. Jack had seen him before—one of the fishermen from the black Jeep. The Jeep he had also seen at the bridge.

He turned back. "I took a hike today," he said.

•

He told her about his foray at midday while she was being pampered. How he had taken his rod for cover and crossed the river and changed boots and climbed the north side of the canyon in the rain. And surveyed the rugged country to the north—mountain ranges cut with creeks, the drainages deep—and how he had crawled to the ledge and scanned their canyon. He told her what he had seen that confused him and made his skin crawl. She watched him, one hand on her cold longneck, and she didn't drink once.

He said, "The fence, that was the first thing. That big crazy contraption of a gate at the lodge—"

"Kinda steampunk, the way it rattles and those cams tip back."

"Yeah, well, they have the same model year at Kreutzer's. No arty cams and no bead-welded trout, but it's the same steel plates, same dimensions, same state of rust—like they were installed the same year by the same crew. Okay, one neighbor gets inspired by another, happens all the time."

She nodded.

"But then I got to looking at the fence."

"The fence?"

"Yeah, have you noticed—" Jack glanced out the plate window; the blond-beard dude in the black cap and shirt was gone. Jack took a swig. God, cold beer tasted good right now. Well, maybe it was nothing, he—they, the guys in the black caps—were nothing. He'd keep an eye out. He turned back. He didn't have to keep his voice down as the happy hour crowd was yelling to each other over "I Love Rock 'n' Roll" by Joan Jett and the Blackhearts. What was it about mountain towns? Why did they always play *the* most obvious music on the planet?

"You were saying? The fence?"

"Yeah, on either side of our gate there's a chain-link. Runs upcanyon to Kreutzer's and down to Ellery's. All hidden from the road by trees. Only place you can see it from the inside is the gravel lot where everybody parks their cars. A mile and a half. Eight feet high, I know, cause it's the height of elk fence. That's a whole crapload of fencing." He drank. A beefy thirty-something in a powder blue polo shirt and a Texans cap squeezed through the crowd carrying a pitcher of beer in one hand and three glasses in another. As he passed their table he looked down at Alison and said, "They sure got sweet snapper in these hills . . ." Jack grimaced, thought about reaching out to stop the man, then shook his head, waved him on. Not worth the trouble. Not now.

"So, the fences?"

Jack tipped the bottle back, emptied and raised it to a waitress by the bar, held up two fingers, nodded thanks. "Okay, so this is prime water, world famous, whatever. Fishermen poach it, sure. Maybe. But this fence, it's like military grade. I mean at home, all it takes is four feet of barbed wire and a little 'Private Property' sign that doesn't mention crap about getting shot."

"Okay."

"Okay, and at the top of this fence are the three strands, barbed wire, on an angle arm. Like they have at prisons and such. You've seen them."

She nodded.

"But here's the weird thing, the angle is facing in. Into the lodge property, in toward the river."

"You mean—" The waitress breezed to the edge of the table with two more bottles and two waters. She swept up the empties, clacked down the cold ones, and set a basket of French fries and a ketchup bottle in the middle.

"Fries?" Jack said.

"And the beer. Some guy in back."

"Black cap?"

"Can't remember. Hey, you're the singer!" the girl said, beaming at Alison. "You're Al—"

Alison put up a hand. "Ha! I wish," she said. "I get that a lot. I actually raise llamas."

The waitress looked unconvinced. "I got you," she said, and put a finger to her mask.

"Damn," Jack said

"What?" Alison said.

"Nothing." He didn't want to freak her out with the men in black—and he forced himself to smile and thank the waitress, who whisked off.

"I actually do raise llamas," Alison said. "I have two at home. And if you don't spit it out and tell me about these damn fences I'm gonna have to break one of your ribs again."

"Yeah—" He lifted the bottle, which was fogged with cold, and clicked hers, bottom to bottom, and drank. "The barbed wire at the top is angled *in*."

He let it digest. She moved her lips around. "You mean as if they were trying to keep people *inside*?"

"I don't think there's an *as if*. I mean, sometimes they'll switch the angle around if there's a property line issue, but that's not what's going on here. The edge of the property is the road. They have plenty of room."

"Whoa."

"Yeah. So that's not the only thing about the fence. I had binocs. I like to bird-watch, too."

She smiled.

"Kreutzer has the same fence on either side of *his* gate. The very same stuff, same setup. And it's also hidden by a screen of trees. And guess what?"

She shook her head. She wasn't scared but she was . . . something. Her greenish eyes were sparking. She was a little flushed and Jack thought he'd never seen a woman as beautiful. "What?" she said.

"Kreutzer's fence runs straight into the lodge fence. No break."

"Okaay . . . like . . ."

"Like it's the same goddamn property."

"No kidding."

"I know. But then I thought, well, could've been the same property once and got split off. Happens all the time."

"Sure."

"But then I saw four cars pull in."

•

They ate the fries. They were both, they discovered, ravenous, despite lobster for lunch. They managed to get the attention of the server and they ordered two dozen oysters—"We have a theme going today," she said. "I can't believe I even *want* oysters at nine thousand feet!" and she squeezed the lemon wedges over all the half shells—and he told her that the first car was a black pickup with a ladder rack, the second was apparently a plumber's van, and the third was a silver gray pickup, no topper. And at the end of the line was a squad car.

"So?"

"So, the first truck was Kurt's, the second truck was Cody's, and the van in the middle was who-the-hell-knows, and it had no windows. At the back, running sweep, was a squad car. Sheriff's department."

Alison had an oyster halfway to her mouth and she set it back on the crushed ice. "Kurt? Kurt? Jensen, you mean? The manager?"

"Yep."

"Fuck a duck."

"Yep."

She closed her eyes and shook her head as if to clear it. "Cody? He's the other guide. Doesn't say much."

"Right."

"But . . . he said . . . Jensen said he couldn't even get into Kreutzer's to complain about the shot. Said he was batshit crazy. Couldn't even call the bastard. I don't . . ." She stopped. She looked at Jack. Intense. He wanted to lean over and kiss her more than anything. She sat up straight and squared herself. Her gears were whirring, Jack could almost hear them. She looked down and noticed a dab of cocktail sauce or ketchup at the ends of several strands of auburn hair. "Can't take her anywhere," she murmured, and dipped a napkin into her water glass and dabbed the hair clean. "It's all BS," she said finally.

"Some of it is," Jack said.

"I'd like to know which part."

"That'd be good," he said, and he thought how he hadn't even told her about the wading boot buried in the trees and the men in black.

•

They ate. The oysters, the fries . . . and as the happy hour crowd became a little more subdued and diluted by serious diners, they ordered skirt steaks French style with more fries, and artichoke salads. The clamor subsided but not much—a lot of the serious partyers stayed on, as they had. Jack cast a glance into the back of the cavernous pub more than once, but couldn't see anyone in a black cap—not a hard man in a black T-shirt. There was one young blond woman in a mixed group of what appeared to be mountain bikers still in their zip shirts and baggy shorts, still, it seemed, amped up and euphoric from their biking. Her black cap said LIVE TO RIDE, and Jack wondered again about a life dedicated to pleasure, and wondered too at the prick of envy he felt watching the loud and laughing group; some were his age, for sure. Because he knew that pleasure alone was a mostly empty vessel. But. Mountain biking with a bunch of friends looked like fun.

He excused himself and made his way back to the restroom and still saw neither of the two men. Maybe they weren't being surveilled, maybe he was getting jumpy.

At the table, Alison had ordered two coffees, black. When he sat, she said, "It's funny, I'm paying, I think, a crazy amount to stay at the lodge. Not sure, 'cause Benny, my manager, takes care of all stuff like that. But I saw his face when I told him I'd read a story about it in *Travel + Leisure* and he looked it up." She grinned. "I like giving him a jolt. But, you know, I feel more relaxed and happy here, in this bar."

Jack did, too.

She blew on the beads of oil on the surface of her coffee, and inhaled the smoky steam, closing her eyes for half a second. When she opened them, she said, "The fishing's different. I just get lost in it. That's another world."

What he always thought. He always marveled how, as soon as he stepped into a creek, the rhythms changed, and all the natural laws governing movement and gravity and light seemed to alter. Light moved differently on the water, and so did he.

He said, "I do, too. Sometimes I forget my name."

"A simple, good name like that?" And she leaned forward and tipped her head to the side and he kissed her. Not long, not deep, but enough, and he knew there had never been a kiss like it in his life. Her skin smelled of summer, and she tasted of coffee and salt, and a sweetness that came from her alone. She pulled back slowly and smiled and this time it was shy, and Jack was struck by how young she looked—as if, when the armor of all those years fell away, the years did, too.

"Well, phew," she said. "We got that over with."

"Yeah, phew," he stammered.

"Want a cognac?" she said.

"Oh yeah. But I'm driving."

She made a face and waved over the server.

After she ordered two Armagnacs he said, "Why don't you just leave?"

"Leave?"

"I mean if the lodge feels somehow off, or creepy."

The question seemed to startle her. "Whew." She blew out. "Well, I can't go home, that's one thing."

"You can't?"

She shook her head. "Nope."

"I didn't mean to intrude."

She smiled again and this time it was sad. "Jack, you probably can't. Intrude. I mean if you tried. There are no signs here saying 'Get the Hell Away, Don't Get Shot!'"

"Okay."

"I just can't go home right now."

"But you could go anywhere."

"I suppose. But this stuff here is just starting to get interesting, don't you think?"

•

It was after ten when they got to the truck. There was still a decent milling of tourists and locals on the streets. Three years ago, when the first novel virus had hit and rocked the country and the world, some of the hottest clusters in the West were these mountain ski towns. Especially the more exclusive resorts like Crested Butte, because they were patronized by rich travelers from Europe who brought the sickness with them. But now, as the first virus had mostly burned itself out and been vaccinated against, and other novel viruses had moved over the world and hit different countries more or less hard, and economies had convulsed and adjusted, those who could afford it spent more and more time on retreat in the remotest places. Like these mountains. The densest cities were still the most dangerous. And vacationing deep in the mountains when possible had become a cultural habit more than anything.

Jack felt just a little warmed up. As they drove out onto the county highway and lost the lights of town behind them, she flipped off the radio and they drove with just the current of air pouring in the windows. A night of stars and cold and neither said much. They drove under the dark bulk of the mountain. When they got to the first bridge and crossed the East River, Alison said over the wind, "Pull over, will you?"

He turned onto a wide shoulder just past the bridge abutment and tugged the stick into neutral and set the brake. He thought she would shove open the door but she sat still as the engine idled.

"I wanna do it again," she said.

"Again? What?" Jack said.

She turned and he could barely see her in the dash lights but he could tell she was making a face—her *Am I talking to a frigging child* expression. She unzipped her short wool jacket.

"The kissing thing."

In the dim light he could see the curve of her breasts in the sheer blouse. She reached up and pushed her long hair back past her ear and now he could see the paleness of her neck, the silver earring, her collarbone, barely. He swallowed. He had sworn he wouldn't unsettle himself now, not this close to everything that had happened; he needed just a little solid ground for just a little while. And he'd screwed it up in the bar. And he liked her more than he'd liked anyone for a long time.

"It's not my M.O.," she said. "I'm pretty shy that way and I like being in my own company a lot."

"I get that," he said.

"But . . ."

"But," he said.

"There's nothing on earth I want more right now than for you to scoot over here and touch me. I don't really care how."

She reached for his hand on the shifter and picked it up and placed it against her ear and he could feel the curve of her jaw and the heat of her neck and she kissed the inside of his wrist. And then she was kissing the soft parts of his palm and then his hand went into her hair and he leaned over and tipped her face up to his. And now there was no crowded pub, no men in black caps, just the two of them in the dark and he was falling. Almost as if into a rock pool from a great height, but it was all warm not cold and he was murmuring and breathing and she was all around him and he was still reaching for her, still falling, and he relinquished himself into her goodness and he went deaf and blind. And so he did not hear the passing car or see if it was a dark late-model Jeep.

CHAPTER SEVEN

Three things happened next that surprised him.

1. When he parked his truck inside the gate at the lodge and they walked down the sandy road to the cabins they did not hold hands or talk, but they walked slowly and their shoulders bumped in a genial rhythm and the aspen rustled. He felt easier in her company than he had in anyone else's for a long time.

2. He slept like a log and dreamless until just before daybreak.

3. At very first light he coasted the cruiser bike down to the lodge. Just when he knew Shay would put out the first pot of coffee. And Cody was sitting on the edge of the porch, not in a chair but on the planks themselves, holding a steaming cup in two hands. He was lanky and loose-jointed even seated, and he had that air of a man squatting beside a campfire. Also he seemed to be listening to the daybreak breeze with his whole body. Jack had grown up with boys who could have been Cody's cousins, or brothers, and he knew when a man was good to have in your outfit and probably dangerous otherwise.

"Morning," Jack said.

Cody swiveled his head. Jack knew Cody had heard the crunch of the bike tires on pine needles, but he only looked up now. "Grab a cup" was all he said.

Jack did. Inside the lodge, no one was at the crackling hearth yet and the lights, the ones that were on, were dimmed. All but the standing lamp by the coffee setup. He liked the quiet. He went to the farthest of the three pots—he didn't read the label, he was getting used to where they kept the dark roast— and he filled a mountain lion mug and walked back out to the porch, sat beside his colleague. The one whose truck had gone right through Kreutzer's big security gate about sixteen hours before. Jack wanted to ask Cody how the fishing was yesterday afternoon, where he had taken the couple, etc., just to see how a kid like this would go about lying. But the wading boot in the spruce duff, the image of it, made him think twice. "Good day yesterday?" was all he said.

Cody shrugged. "Like every other pretty much."

They were looking at the stocked fish pond ringed with aspen. No trout rose but a fat kingfisher sat on a dead limb almost over the water. It was a perfect perch and Jack wondered if the management didn't cut it for a reason. Maybe it was entertaining to watch the bird hunt.

"You?" Cody said.

"Good. It's good water."

"About as fine as any mountain stream you'll ever fish, I'd say. Except for Tomichi Creek, where you're going today."

"I am?"

"Yep. Jensen told me to tell you. Pack a lunch. Alison K marked it down for day three." Cody stuck two fingers in the zip breast pocket of his Carhartt and fished out a key. It was on a marlin keychain, which seemed weird. But then Den probably had a fishing lodge in Barbados. The tail was a bottle opener. "There's two gates, same lock."

"What's the opener for?"

"Mr. Den says it's for cracking the Guinness when the client catches the biggest brown they've ever seen. I guess he never opened a bottle with the back of a knife."

"Huh."

From the same pocket Cody fingered out a folded slip of paper. "Here's the directions. Simple but you'll need to know the mileage from the turnoff. No cell service out there, either, so don't bother mapping it. Also, there's a new couple coming this afternoon. You'll meet 'em at the bar before dinner." Now Cody looked straight at Jack. The same flat gray eyes. Wolfish in their watchfulness. Dispassionate, and holding distances Jack bet no one had ever traveled. Cody said, "You haven't been to happy hour much."

"Just getting settled is all."

Cody didn't comment. He turned back to look at the pond. He sipped his coffee.

"Is Jensen gonna guide?" Jack said.

Cody winced. "Jensen?"

"Yeah. Is he gonna guide?"

"Jensen doesn't guide."

"Who's gonna guide the new couple?"

Cody didn't say anything. He watched the pond. After a while he said, "Maybe they don't wanna fish. Some folks come just for the peace and quiet."

Peace and quiet, Jack thought. Shots fired, and snarling mastiffs, and barn owls. But he kept his mouth shut.

Cody stood. "Refill?" he said.

"I'm good," Jack said. "I'll get one in a minute."

He watched the pond. Gray green glass with tendrils of mist coming off the water. A spreading ring, now two, as of passing rain—the quiet feeding of a trout. The kingfisher held his perch. Jack heard the yaw of a screen door and he looked to his right, past the porch, and saw Shay come out of the back door of the kitchen carrying steel food trays, two stacked. She was wearing a maroon Arc'teryx softshell and a light knitted wool cross-country ski hat cocked jauntily on her forehead. She didn't see him. She loaded the trays into the back of a golf cart parked there and pulled open the screen door again and disappeared inside. A moment later she came out with two more trays, loaded them on top of the others, then went back for two stainless insulated coffee urns like the ones inside, and a large carafe of orange juice. She packed those, too, climbed into the cart, and drove onto the track on the far side of the pond. The cart bumped silently on its electric motor up into the aspen. Jack knew that the cart path climbed the hill and passed behind the main office house and linked to the parking lot by the gate. On the far side of which were equipment and supply sheds. The carts were used by the housecleaning and maintenance staff, and apparently by servers like Shay.

Kingfishers are easily startled. Jack had fished with them all his life, and he liked how they would perch upstream and watch him work a creek—he liked to think it was one fisher observing another—but as soon as he waded up just a few feet to cast for new water they were off: a downward lilting arc with a swoop up to the next perch. And repeat. They were good company and he had fished with a single bird for miles. But Jack noticed that this bird did not even flinch as Shay drove the golf cart past his chosen tree: this was the bird's territory and he must have watched her enact this ritual every morning and he was used to her.

The trays were the steel flats used by caterers and schools and made to slide into racks. The same used at the Orvis fishing camp in the Adirondacks he and Wynn had worked before their Canada trip three years ago. He figured Shay had loaded at least a score of breakfasts.

Were they for staff? He doubted it. As he had geared up in the mornings he had heard the sounds of cars entering the gate for the day's work and later noticed the dozen vehicles parked next to his. Most of the workers except maybe Jensen, who seemed to live on the property somewhere, arrived having eaten already. Huh.

Jack heard the latch behind him and the clomp of packer boots and Cody sat beside him again at the edge of the porch. Didn't say a word. Ten or fifteen minutes passed. Two young guides enjoying their first cup and just watching the dawn drain the last pockets of darkness out of the canyon. *What could be better than this?* Jack said it to himself, his mantra, and he tasted the coffee and then watched as Shay in her cart reemerged from the trees on the far side of the pond and swung in beside the kitchen door. She lifted her hand to Cody and then did a double take as she noticed Jack sitting right behind him. And she waved again, but tentatively. Jack waved back.

Had Shay seemed startled? Yes. He noted it. Noted it along with every other messed-up detail and sign. Sign of what? He had no idea. But they were starting to stack up.

•

Breakfast was faster than usual. Cody ate with his golden couple out on the deck, beside the open fire. Jack glanced out there a few times and thought they seemed dulled again—no quick smiles and easy laughter, no spirited hand gestures of a caffeine-fueled story. She wore a long-billed fishing cap for the first time, pulled down low. Noted. Will and Neave ate at their table closest to the hearth, as far away as they could be from him and Alison K. They barely nodded a greeting, and they had dark circles under their eyes as if bruised, and again he thought they looked hungover.

He and Alison ate with gusto and didn't say much. Not out of any awkwardness, but because they didn't have to. He had never felt such easy concord with a woman. Not that he had a ton of experience. After he'd broken it off with Cheryl he'd been with a couple of girls at Dartmouth, but they were flings, he guessed. One was kindled on an outing club wilderness ski trip up in the college grant just before Christmas, a week of cutting cross-country ski tracks through deep woods and camping beside iced-over brooks. So cold even the ledge drops were frozen, and they'd used an axe to break the glass beneath them. She was Margaret, a generous-spirited New Hampshire girl who had grown up with horses as he had, and he thought he might love her. It had lasted into March, until she'd had to leave school for good to take care of her dying mother. Jack had never understood why she'd broken it off; he had a truck, after all, he could've driven over a couple of days a week. The other was pure spring fever, a senior who had chatted him up during a bluegrass hoedown at his friend Andy's cabin. Andy was a nut—a hellacious rock and ice climber, banjo player, and brilliant engineer who did zero anything by the book. Jack had met him at the first outing club meeting he and Wynn had attended freshman fall. There were maybe forty students seated around this giant cedar table, and Andy started whispering to Jack French Canadian jokes told in accent. Jack the introvert had been charmed and responded with some of Uncle Lloyd's cowboy jokes. They both laughed so hard they'd gotten kicked out. Andy's truck was outside and he had a six of PBR on the front seat and they'd driven down to the river and polished it off and told the rest of their jokes and stories with appropriate levels of volume and were fast friends after that. Andy graduated that spring and got a job just upriver at the US Army's cryogenic research lab and often invited Jack and Wynn out to his place for dinners and music nights. Usually seven or eight showed up with instruments and it was either bluegrass or old-time country à la Merle Haggard. The group was outside on a late April night playing "Ramblin' Fever," and Jack was leaning against the cabin wall with a Dos Equis, and the singers were lofting into the chorus when he heard a contralto to his right and he practically bumped into the prettiest girl he had seen since he'd left Colorado. Pretty like I'm-going-to-Duke-Medical-School-and-I-can-run-seven-minute-miles-through-hills pretty. That had lasted just over a month until she'd graduated.

But this was different. Very. Suddenly he wasn't making an effort, not any at all, and he didn't feel in her company like he was some stranger to himself.

They ate breakfast fast; threw his pack, a small cooler, and their fishing gear into the back of his truck and drove out to the bottomland ranch and the slow, winding blackwater creek.

•

They fished for four hours straight. Like many creeks that meander through the broader valleys of the West, the private upper stretch of the Tomichi twisted on itself and twisted back in a series of looping bites as if resisting with every turn its surrender to a larger stream. It would take its own sweet time and nose into every oxbow and never offer a view past the next tight bend. Jack thought it was like reading some of the South American novelists who drove him crazy and whom he couldn't stop enjoying. How their stories twisted and mazed and got lost in themselves. On Tomichi, the same intractable spirit wound the stream through thick walls of willows and alders. The thinnest margin of gravel bar here and there, but mostly the brush was overhanging. It was hard wading and there was no place at all to stretch out a cast. It was as if God had designed a creek to harbor the balkiest brown trout on earth. Jack had heard stories of some truly great fishers getting skunked out here.

At least there was no wind to speak of. The clouds blew by on their own cold currents and striped the bends with shadow, but down on the water the dark pools were nearly glass. And the morning warmed fast and the hatches drifted up and sparked in sunlight; and with a few tips from Jack, Alison got her roll cast going and flipped her nymphs across the creek without snagging the brush.

She hummed, and he relished the professional distance he kept between them as she fished. Sometimes she sang to herself. And it was strange—her voice was so rich, and broke so sweet, and seemed to flow past itself in layers like sliding water—and there was so much truth in it, and pain—he felt that it wreathed him. He didn't need to touch her. He stayed back the guide's four feet and he enjoyed just watching: she kept a rhythm in her casts, and in the stripping in of line, and in her steps forward, as if she were using the music in her head to keep time.

They ate lunch in the sun on the one sandbar broad enough to sit on. He bit into the chicken salad on toast and inhaled the slow-water tannin scent of the creek. The light gleamed off the narrow leaves of the willows the way it does only in late August. They shared a bottle of ginger kombucha and then shared another.

In the early afternoon they saw the silent rings of the trout dapping the surface and after that she casted a single light dry fly. She flipped it backhand up under the branches and let the tiny pale tuft touch the water as if blown on the breeze.

"Pure," she said over her shoulder. "Feels pure."

"All fishing's pure," Jack said.

"Right, if it's so pure we don't need to get grandiose and talk about it."

"What I was going to say."

She caught fish. Not many, but one brown that seemed to fill the net with such muscular defiance Jack released it with relief and a quiet salute.

As the sun lowered over the Sawtooths they turned to each other and without a word they packed it in. They found a break in the brush and pushed through. They climbed over a sagging barbed-wire fence, and followed the ruts of a four-wheel track through sage and wheatgrass back to the truck. Warmer here than in the canyon. They sat on the tailgate and pried off the wading boots and then stood on the dirt and pushed and tugged off the waders one leg at a time.

"What could be better than this?" Jack murmured.

"What?"

"What I always try to tell myself. What could be better than this?" He was sitting on the tailgate and she was standing on one leg wrestling to get the wet neoprene sock of her wader over her heel. She glanced up at him and blew a strand of hair off her face and her greenish eyes were lit in the long sun.

"I like that," she said. "Why do you have to *try* to tell yourself?"

Jack shrugged and reached beside him and pried off the lid of the cooler with one hand and dug a can out of the ice. "Hawaiian Punch. I'm sure there's beer in here."

"I'll take it," she said, and reached a hand out unsteadily, still on one leg like a heron. "Thanks. That was pretty special." She raised the can. "And this is the hardest part of fishing, for sure—getting off the waders."

"Hold on." Jack hopped down. "I forgot my job." He knelt beside her and she bent the wadered knee and held her foot back like a horse waiting to have her hoof picked, and he tugged on the bootie and almost pulled her off balance, and then he set a hand on the back of her hip and tugged again. She was wearing black workout tights and there was nothing underneath them. He pulled the wader down and off and then she turned around. The hand that had been on her hip slipped over the rise and fall of her pelvis as she turned, and he was looking straight into a pitch of black nylon and the sheen of it off the swell of her pubis, and then he felt her hand on the top of his head. He felt dizzy.

"Um," she said.

"Um." He wanted her, and he didn't. She was a superstar celebrity. Wynn had dated into a celebrity family once and it had not gone at all well. Jack knew that he'd end up being out of place and a burden for Alison, and he didn't want to be a burden to anyone. Ever.

She cleared her throat. "I . . . I feel . . ." Her voice was husky. "You . . ." She stopped. She tapped the top of his head and when he looked up she was smiling. "You are . . . well . . . I could write a song about you. More than one."

He smiled back at her now. Her smoky, musky scent was intoxicating. "And," she said, "I'm paying you. Which feels weird. I don't really wanna be that gal."

Jack was surprised at the wave of relief. "Okay," he said.

"Okay. So turn around if you want. I'm gonna try to get these tights off."

•

They sat on the tailgate in the lowering sun. They drank Hawaiian Punch happily, in the hum of endorphins and relaxed tiredness that can come after a full day fishing. Jack couldn't hear the reticent creek, though it was just beyond the screen of willows, but he heard the evening trill of a meadowlark. It was unabashed and self-delighting. One of his favorite songs. She said, "I don't wanna go back."

"You don't?" he said. "To the lodge?"

"Not right now."

Jack checked his watch. "Four-oh-five. We'll barely make it to the bar before dinner if we leave now." He meant the bar at the lodge.

"Fuck the bar. Will and Neave can barely speak anymore. Those others, the blondies, they looked kinda beat-up this morning, too. Jeez."

"I noticed that."

"What the hell? What's going on? Will and Neave don't fish, the Youngens fish, supposedly, but we never see them on the river." She rolled down the sleeves of her quick-dry shirt and buttoned the wrists. "Any ideas?"

Jack said, "This morning, just before you showed up for coffee, I saw Shay loading maybe twenty breakfasts into the back of one of those golf carts. On trays."

"Twenty?"

"Just guessing. More than ten."

"Who would she be taking them to?"

"She was heading upstream. That's one thing. The little cart path goes to the parking area inside the gate. So either to a vehicle or on upriver."

"To Kreutzer's."

"It's only half a mile more."

Alison chewed her bottom lip. "It's like it's another lodge. Like maybe they have a bunch of guests there, too, but for some reason we're not supposed to know about it."

"Yeah, right. I keep thinking about the boot."

"The boot?"

Jack's mouth closed. He had forgotten that he hadn't told her.

"What boot?"

"I don't want to freak you out. A guide's supposed to keep certain things to himself."

"What thing have you kept to yourself? I'd say you've been free with all your things lately."

He laughed, couldn't help it. Last night in the truck seemed like a dream. Now she shook her hair out of her cap and it was a mess and she looked righteous and pleased with herself. "Point taken," he said.

"So stop being coy. Is this how cowboys are?"

"When you caught your fish by Kreutzer's and I went across the river to pee, I saw a boot."

"So?"

"Just the edge of it. Sticking out of a bed of spruce needles. All hidden in those thick trees. The ground had been disturbed. It was a wading boot."

She didn't say anything.

"The ground around it had been roughed up, about the size of a tent. Or a grave. So that night I went back. I went to the same spot, I'm dead sure. There was no boot and the ground had been smoothed over. That's when I heard the scream."

"The owl."

"The owl." Jack blinked at her, into the sun. "The guide I've been hired to replace left in a hurry was what Kurt told me."

"Kurt. Kurt Jensen."

"Right."

"Mr. Kurt has an interesting relationship with the truth," she said.

"That's what's dawning on me."

Her eyes darkened. They were pretty when they were lit, but when a shadow moved into them they were so beautiful they stopped his breath. "Are you saying . . . ?"

"I'm not saying anything," he said. "I just wonder if you shouldn't check out. Maybe say you've been called back to Nashville or wherever for urgent business."

"Asheville."

"Asheville?"

"Mountains of North Carolina. I like to fish, remember?"

"So, Asheville. Maybe you shouldn't finish out the week—"

"Ten days."

"A lot can happen."

"You chew, right?" she said.

He nodded.

"Let me have some."

"You?"

"Singer can't smoke. Shouldn't."

He fished the tin out of the back pocket of his Wranglers, handed it over.

Jack said, "Did Mr. Den say his first name? When you talked to him?"

"Sure. His name's Nicholas. Nick."

Out of a front pocket, Jack now slid his phone. "No cell service. Let's go."

"Where?"

"Back toward town. I have an idea."

She didn't say "You do?" She reached in the back of the truck where she had folded a fleece vest. "What's in the bucket?" she said.

"Fencing tools. I leave it in there out of habit."

She tipped it toward her. "Fencing tools, come-along, can of staples . . ."

"How do you know that stuff?"

"Country girl, remember?"

"Hunh."

"Dynamite? Three sticks?"

"Don't you have bedrock in North Carolina? Places on the ranch even the Hulk couldn't dig a post."

She turned her face back into the sun and her eyes lit and her laugh challenged the meadowlark.

•

They didn't get decent cell reception until they were nearly three miles from town, so she said they might as well go in and have a beer. He said they'd be lucky to make the lodge dinner at all at this rate and she said, Fuck it, we might as well just eat in Crested Butte while we're at it. He asked if that wouldn't raise suspicion, and she said, Of what? That we're boinking? And he laughed and she said as they drove that it must happen all the time, the guide-client thing, and they'd probably be suspicious if they weren't. She was right, probably, but Jack still felt uneasy. He had the feeling, with no evidence to support it, that the lodge did not take kindly to guides and guests going AWOL. But she was paying the bill, what were they going to do? Fire her? His elbow was out the window and he shivered but it wasn't from cold.

The town was less packed tonight and they parked right on Elk and walked a block down to the Dogwood. They couldn't get their old table, but they got the four-top next to it in the window, and the waitress saw them from the bar and lifted her chin, turned herself sideways in the crowd, and raised her tray to get through. She recognized them and put down waters and unhooked the mask from one ear to reveal a big smile. "Blowdowns?" she said.

"Yep," Alison said. "Good memory."

"Eating?" the girl said. She was beaming again, as if she didn't at all believe the llama-raising story.

"Definitely."

"Okay, I'm Molly. Back in a sec with the beers." She took two narrow happy hour menus out of her apron pocket, slid them onto the table, and dove back into the crowd.

"So much for social distancing," Alison said.

"Right?"

"What was your idea?" she said.

"Hold on, I'll come around." Jack moved to the seat beside her and pulled out his phone.

•

There was a candle in a glass on the table and Alison took out an ancient Zippo. Jack loved the snick and scrape of the old lighters as they opened. Uncle Lloyd had one with which he fired up a cigar once in a while.

"Ambiance," she said, and lit the candle.

"I thought you didn't smoke," Jack said.

"Nope, the lighter was Papa's. It's good luck." She showed it to him. The nickel plating was worn to black at the edges and was stamped with a Harley on one side and a white-tailed deer on the other. "His two passions," she said. "And me, of course."

They googled Mr. Nicholas Den. There was a Scot whose Spanish land-grant ranch, the Royal Rancho, comprised most of Santa Barbara County in 1880, but that wasn't him. Then there was a Trinity College, Oxford, and Yale PhD biochemist who now lived in London and had invented synthetic RNA, whatever that was. His company, DenGen—Nicholas clearly had a sense of fun— was bought by the German agri-pharma giant BauerSpahn for . . .

"Holy crap." Alison squinted into the phone and pressed her icy beer bottle against the side of her face.

"Two-point-one billion dollars," Jack said.

"And stock, worth half a billion more."

She squinted again into the phone. "Dddddddddddddd—reading sounds . . ." she said. She read faster than he did. "Okay listen to this," she said. "He was a major investor in PreVen—the dude can't help himself, I'm surprised it wasn't called PreVenDen—a Dutch company that was working on a promising vaccine for Covid Redux. It failed in its second clinical trial."

"That's Wiki. Let's go back."

Jack scrolled down the pages of search hits for Den. Awards, DenGen announcements, conference speaking engagements—Den had spoken all over the world about the medical and industrial potential of synthetic RNA, which included medical therapeutics and gene analysis. "Funny, there's nothing recent about Den and the Kingfisher Lodge. Hold on." Jack searched for the lodge and found the usual reams of promotional hits, articles in *Travel + Leisure,* in the American Express Platinum magazine *Departures,* testimonials from world-class fly fishermen and -women.

"Hey," Jack said. "Apparently he's got more than one. Fancy five-star fishing lodge. Here in *Traveler* it says, 'just one of the premier lodges in the Seven collection.' Seven, that's the company. Damn."

"Go back to Den," Alison said. He did. He flipped back to page nine of hits and rolled down with his thumb, snagged on something, scrolled back. Jack recited: "Simba, beloved red lion of Hwange National Park, shot by biomedical pioneer Nicholas Den. Special permit awarded by the government of Zimbabwe. The *Los Angeles Times*."

He clicked on the link and they put their heads together and read in silence beside the big window. Out on the street tourists streamed by, the sky over the brightly painted wooden houses deepened into a bowl of clearest blue. In the bar, the gregarious babble around them did not cease. A plate of cheese nachos slipped in front of them and they looked up and Molly was grinning. "On the house." She swapped their empties with fresh cold ones. "These I've gotta charge for." Jack looked up and touched his cap, *Thanks*. He felt lucky in Alison's company. He thought they must project something good together, out here in the world. Back at the lodge it was different; back there, he was feeling more and more . . . what? Suspect maybe. Isolated. And he didn't know why.

"Bastard," Alison muttered. "No words. Look, he worked with the Hwange Conservation Project to reopen lion hunting in the park. Rationale given that revenue from the few pricey permits would bankroll conservation efforts. Un-frigging-believable. Look at the smarmy sonofabitch." She reached with a finger and tapped the news photo. There was Den, a handsome rogue, dark-haired, lean, hint of a smile, squatting with his rifle under a savannah tree and holding up the head of the gorgeous lion with the glorious ruddy mane.

"Can I scroll back?" Jack said.

She nodded.

"Created quite a stink. Not much in the news after that," Jack said. "Looks like he and his publicists decided he better lay low for a while."

"Let's go," she said. She tipped back the new beer and drank half, clacked it down on the wood table.

"Right now?"

"Yes." Alison dug two twenties out of her jeans and set them under the wet beer. "I wanna go to the bar at the lodge. I wanna meet this new couple you mentioned. What time is it?"

"Five fifteen."

"Okay, you better drive like you mean it."

•

He drove back fast with the warm evening rushing in the open windows and the country station turned all the way up. They dropped off the aspen ridge and thumped over the bridge and turned up the Taylor River and just before they entered the canyon, in an open bottomland of meadows and cottonwoods, they saw a figure running up the road. A slight figure in white—a white robe? A *hospital* gown? As they passed they saw it was a thin black-haired girl. Her face was scratched and she looked wild and panicked and she was in a hospital gown and she was barefoot. Alison craned her head out the window and looked back and yelled, "What the hell?" But they were already around the bend.

Jack pulled over into the purple asters and overgrown grass of the shoulder. "We gotta . . ."

"Check it out," she yelled over him. He spun the wheel and lurched forward and cranked a three-point turn. He gunned it back onto the pavement and they came around the bend and Alison popped off the radio and cried, "Wha—?"

Pulled up on the opposite shoulder was a squad car, lights flashing, and a deputy in a tan uniform was out in the road wrestling the girl. He had her bodily in the air and he slammed her against his hood and the gown shifted and they could see her bare bottom and then he had one arm and then the other twisted back and he was cuffing her. Just then he looked up and saw them. He waved, nodded, like *All under control now, thanks for stopping,* and he put his hand on the top of her head and as gently as he could he settled her into the back seat. Then he got in the front, pulled closed the door that said GUNNISON COUNTY SHERIFF, and pulled back onto the county highway. And then he did something that surprised them both: he didn't turn around and head back to town. Instead he accelerated up the canyon, the way they were going, and was around the bend and gone.

"What the heck was that?" Alison said.

"Beats me. Maybe the newest virus, I don't even know what they call the latest one. Maybe it was someone breaking some sort of quarantine."

"Yeah," Alison said. "That's probably what it was. They have quarantine centers in the damndest places." But she forgot to turn on the music again as they drove back, and she was quiet and thoughtful the whole way.

•

Neither of them showered. They had to pass the little path down to Jack's cabin on the walk to the lodge, so they just dumped the pack and their fishing gear onto his porch. He held open the screen for her and they both splashed off in his sink and she pulled her thick hair back into a band and they went on down the track. "*Listo* beasto," she said. He carried the little lunch cooler, that was it.

At the bar it was as festive as Jack's first night. The mood swings were jarring. They pushed through the heavy door from the porch into a room alive with conversation and the smells of rum and fresh baked biscuits. The Cuban *son* "Candela" poured from hidden speakers. Will and Neave were on stools at the corner looking just as rich but much more rested and energized. Next to them were the fleecy blond Youngens, laughing and talking loudly—the days of proximity seemed to have finally created some sense of cohort. Cody was there, too, beyond them, unsmiling but not unhappy, with a longneck in front of him. And all of their attention was turned to the new blood, a very attractive—Jack would have to say beautiful—young couple. They might have been thirty. She wore a simple, snow white button-down longsleeve that might have been a fishing shirt, and it so contrasted with the straight fall of her glossy black hair it was impossible not to stare. Her olive skin was tan, as if she'd recently spent days outside. He was compact and lean in a tailored khaki shirt and had an easy smile. Jack noticed right away that they both moved with a perfect comfort in their own skins and that their eyes were intelligent and curious. They carried a certain authority he sensed was rarely but deftly administered. At least they looked like fisherpeople. As he and Alison stepped to the bar, Ginnie called out, "The wayfaring strangers! Brilliant! Welcome. I think you two would fish twenty-four hours if there was some way to forgo sleep. Everybody, Jack and Alison. Jack and Alison, this is Yumi and Teiji—" The new couple turned on their stools and lowered their heads in a slight bow.

Well, now we're getting somewhere, Jack thought. At last this looks like a fishing lodge.

Ginnie called, "Pull up a stool over here." She gestured to the other side of the new guests and tagged them each with the forehead thermometer. "Jack, I've got your number"—she was already lifting an ice-cold Cutthroat ale from under the bar. "Alison, love, beer or"—she waved her hand over a line of mint-garnished tumblers—"can I sell you tonight's mojito special?"

•

He almost managed to forget. The wider context. Sometimes the company is so congenial, the day's fishing so glorious, the music and the drinks so spot-on . . . and the wonderful sense of having a new ally so restful and invigorating at once . . . it was easy to forget. Yumi and Teiji were charming. They were just to his left, and they broke away from the main conversation for a few minutes to ask Alison and Jack about the day's fishing. Amid the telling, and in their few but carefully considered questions, the new couple betrayed a thoughtfulness and knowledge that went beyond politeness. They clearly took fishing seriously and were not here just for the peace and quiet.

•

Alison invited the two to join them for dinner. The four sat at the table by the window overlooking the river and the snowy rapid below. The sun was settling into the V of the canyon downstream and the river funneled and held the sprayed light. It warmed the pines and flushed the sandstone rimrock and gleamed in the lush greens of the alders and box elders at water's edge. Again Jack thought, *There is no more than this.* But there was. Shay brought out a chilled Chardonnay to pair with tonight's Cornish hen, and she held the bottle in a wrapped cloth for inspection by the guests, all of whom nodded amiably, and when she got to Jack her eyes slid away.

The conversation moved easily from fishing to when everybody arrived and where they were from. The new couple had flown from their mountain house outside of Sendai in the north of Japan's main island—they had the house because they loved to ski in winter almost as much as they loved to fish—and did Jack, the Colorado native, know that the snow in northern Japan had been compared favorably to the champagne powder of Colorado and Utah?

"Of course," Yumi interjected, perfectly timed so as not to interrupt her husband, "nothing in the world can compare to the majesty and the distances of the Rocky Mountains."

The distances. Charming. She meant actual square miles, Jack thought, but there were distances here Jack suspected did not exist even in the Himalaya, and they had something to do with how the mountains lived in the imaginations of the people who grew up among them. Jack recalled aloud that Sendai was in the Tohoku region, wasn't it? Made famous by Bashō's *Narrow Road to the Deep North*, and Yumi raised an eyebrow and Teiji cocked his head to the side and studied Jack anew.

"Do you know it? The greatest work of the greatest haiku master?" Teiji asked.

"Yes. I have it with me. I keep an apple box of my favorite books in my truck." Jack rarely betrayed his erudition, but he had never met anyone outside of college who knew anything about Bashō, much less anyone who knew the actual physical territory, and he felt himself getting excited.

"Really?" Yumi said. "So you are an admirer of the poetry of our Green Peach?"

Yes, Jack thought. More than an admirer. And he knew that Green Peach was one of the master's early nicknames, taken in deep respect for Li Po, who lived nine hundred years before, and whose name translated from Chinese as "White Plum." The only course he and Wynn had ever taken together was a class on Japanese poetry. It had been hands down Jack's favorite class. But Jack just said, "Yes."

Teiji, it was clear, was a very polite and considerate man. But he was intrigued now, and he evidently wanted to know if Jack was a name-dropper or a serious reader. And so he laid his fork upside down on the edge of his arugula salad plate and said, "Do you have a favorite haiku?"

Jack laid his own fork aside. "I love many. Honestly, it depends what mood I'm in."

Teiji nodded, as if acknowledging a well-played point in tennis. "Which one would suit you now, for example?"

Jack cleared his throat. Alison watched the two closely, fascinated. Jack seemed more like a kid than she had ever seen him. His guard was down. "Gimme a minute," Jack murmured. "Please." He closed his eyes for just a second, as if trying to hear the vanishing song of a bird. When he opened them he said, "Tonight I'd have to say: *The temple bell ceases— / but the sound continues to toll / out of the flowers.*"

"Bravo!" Yumi cried, and made rapid claps with flattened palms. "I love this poem, too."

Teiji was smiling as if he'd been rooting for Jack the whole time, which he probably had. Jack looked down at his bread plate shyly. He thought, *You don't know that it suits me now because the sounds that stop, but keep resonating, are not always lovely.*

•

"Do you know Bashō?" Yumi said sweetly to Alison, making sure she was not excluded from the conversation.

Alison smiled, Jack thought, with some mischief. "Not too much," she said. "I've heard of him. My neighbor has the one about the frog and the pond chiseled on his gatepost."

Well, she was charming them, too. She was sticking with her salt-of-the-earth, mountains-of-Carolina persona, which, Jack thought, was exactly who she was.

By the vichyssoise, they were talking about the newest coronavirus. The latest one that was moving across Central Asia and had already arrived in Beijing and the US. It was not as deadly as the one that had ripped through South Asia two falls ago, but it was of grave concern because it seemed to be mutating faster than the others. Teiji averred that Japan, of course, was a leader in testing and real-time tracking, and had managed to isolate and contain most outbreaks in the past few years. Alison said that the US did not have nearly the sophistication or precision of identifying who was immune and who was vulnerable through each wave, perhaps because of the sprawl of the country, but also because of its culture of lionizing individualism, and she thought that people here were almost resigned to having novel and not-so-novel coronavirus seasons the way we have flu seasons.

"But of course the mortality rates are much much lower, now that we've all speeded up the production of therapies and vaccines. So it really is almost like the flu."

"Of course," Yumi said politely, and her husband politely nodded.

By the time they were served the fresh Maine blueberries in cream and maple syrup, and Cognac, which all declined, and decaf coffee, which all took, Jack understood that this considerate and modest couple were a team to be reckoned with, and he bet they were exceptionally good trout fishers.

•

Jack excused himself after the first cup of coffee, and thanked Yumi and Teiji for the company. He said he had some gear to organize before bed, traded a quick *to be continued* glance with Alison, and stood.

He went out the heavy door into the icy star-filled dark—clear again, this time probably frost—and on the porch he turned right instead of left.

He had never smoked but he wished he did now. So he'd have an excuse to stand outside the kitchen's back door and take in the night. He knew that Shay smoked back there though she wasn't supposed to. It was one of the first things Kurt had said to him after shaking hands—no smoking on the premises any-where. Private time on the river was the one exception. He had nothing against his guides smoking a cigar or whatever as they fished on an evening off. What could be better, right?

When Kurt said it, Jack had looked up sharply at the enlist-ment of his mantra, though he understood that the manager was using it more as a rhetorical weapon than a prayer . . . He also knew that Shay liked to step out back and walk around the west side of the lodge and chuck grease or greasy water over the bank. Though he doubted she was allowed to do that, either. But he'd wait anyway. It was still early enough, he wasn't going to lose any sleep. He zipped up his down sweater and leaned against the logs by the back door.

He looked up and saw the great canted W of Cassiopeia surfing the trees of the low ridge to the north, and above it the Little

Dipper swinging from its handle around the North Star. Hard to get lost in a place where so many of the nights are clear. If you move at night. And that made him think about the river and the bridge and if anyone at all was really monitoring the cameras in the middle of the night. And Kreutzer's—what was the security perimeter like around that lodge? If there really was anything beyond a heavy gate and tall fence—and perhaps a crazy old coot looking out one of his windows through a spotting scope. Though he doubted that story more and more. And as he let his eyes wander along the ridge eastward, upstream, and tried to capture the constellations that swam there in the net of his knowledge—admittedly not vast in the realm of astronomy; he knew a handful of the most prominent connect-the-dot figures—he thought of his father.

What would Pop be doing now, under these same stars? Probably reading at the kitchen table and not seeing anything beyond the plate window but the reflection of his own lamp, and his own face maybe above the book—a man not yet fifty wearing his granny reading glasses that Jack teased him about, a man not old but going gray, from grief probably, and dashed hopes.

He wondered how his father thought of that morning on the Encampment fourteen years before. How he would remember the four horses stringing along the steep rocky slope in thick trees above the roaring gorge. His father was first on Dandy, the old outfitting horse who never ruffled, leading the flighty half-Arab BJ on a loose rope with the packs; and then his mother on sweet big-boned Mindy, because he, Jack, at eleven decided this morning he wanted to ride sweep. Did Pop remember the sounds as Jack did? The dainty *click* of Dandy's hooves as he crossed the sloping granite slab, the *cluck* as Pop encouraged him to cross, the gentle tug on the lead rope to the packhorse and then: the toss of bit rings and struck stone as BJ startled at something and balked back. And his mother. The gust of alarm: Mindy already halfway across, having to bunch back, too, behind the startled Arab. He would never forget the sharp scrape of Mindy's scrabbling hooves as she lost her footing on tilted rock, his mother up in the stirrups and forward over her neck urging the horse to hold to the slope, trying to get her up in the steep duff above the slab, the thunder of the rapid in the narrow chasm too far below. How the horse scrabbled and slid backward and went over the edge, the two of them for a moment suspended, it seemed, in midair. He saw them hit the white torrent. For a moment, miraculously, they were swimming, she was grabbing for the saddle, then they went over what must have once been a ledge but was now the hump of a breaking wave that rolled down into the trench of a thundering backward-breaking hydraulic, they vanished, came up once, first the mare's dark head, then his mother's arm before they slammed into the wall and were tugged around the bend.

For years afterward he dreamt that the moment she fell and hit the air she took flight. She and the horse both did, and lifted and flew over the other side of the gorge. Her favorite bird had been the great horned owl. "What do you think he's saying tonight?" she would ask Jack whenever they heard one. And for years afterward, whenever one of the huge owls flew over him at night, he believed it was she, gliding by to touch him, to remind him that she loved him.

No owl now. Jack swallowed and breathed. A cigarette would be good, really good, right now. Or one of those mojitos he wasn't allowed to drink because he was a guide limited to two beers;

or how about a mojito without any of the fancy limeade and mint parts, just straight rum, that would be good, too. He was thinking about that when he heard the latch of the door; yellow light fanned across the packed sand where they had parked the golf cart and he heard Shay's hoarse laugh, as she said, "That sure as shit is not happening, Gionno, but thanks for holding the door!" and she backed out into the night carrying a twelve-quart stainless pot and pirouetted and gasped. She was almost face-to-face with Jack.

•

"Whoa, sorry," he said.

"Man, you scared the crap out of me. Lucky this thing is half-full."

"Let me take it."

"I got it. Be right back. Meanwhile you think of a good excuse for being here." She disappeared around the corner and he knew she was tossing whatever was in the pot down the slope. He bet she did it just to get outside, and just to do something—one thing—not allowed.

"That's not allowed, is it?" Jack said when she came back. "Jensen would be mad."

"Nope and yep," she said, and put the pot down on a patch of grass. "This isn't allowed, either." She dug in the front pocket of her tight Wranglers and pulled out a hard pack of Marlboros. She held it out to Jack. Her sleeves were rolled up and he caught sight of the little anchor tattoo on the inside of her wrist. "You?" she said.

"Thanks." Why not? he thought.

"You're gonna work here, you better take up smoking and drinking."

"Yeah?"

She fingered a lighter out of the same pocket and struck the flint, cupped her hand for Jack, then lit her own, inhaled deeply. "Tight damn ship," she said. "Too tight. Have you noticed?"

"Oh, yeah."

"More things not allowed than are." She blew out to the side. "Let's see, what's allowed? Working your ass off, or . . . fishing, eating, being a billionaire. Kurt's certainly not gonna tell Sir William Barron not to smoke on his porch."

"Sir?"

"Knight of the British Empire. Bona fide."

"No shit. He doesn't have an accent."

" 'Cept when he gets tanked. You haven't seen that yet."

"Nope. What'd he get knighted for?"

"Designing a wind turbine that wouldn't turn to matchsticks in a North Sea hurricane."

"Whoa. What about her?"

"Dunno, Neave never says anything. It's quite the clientele. You seem to be enjoying your fishing buddy." She flicked the ash, surveyed the stars. When she looked at him again her eyes were moist. "I could use something stronger, you?"

"Better not. Gotta be on my game in the morning."

"Huh. Everyone here's on their game all the time. Trying to improve themselves. That's what this place is all about."

"It is?"

She didn't say anything. She held the cigarette in the corner of her mouth and from the same magic pocket she pried out a small vial. She shook the white powder into the pocket between thumb and forefinger and snorted, blinked, wiped her nose, and shoved back the bottle. She was a pro. Now she blinked the wetness out of her eyes.

"Better."

Jack didn't say anything. Shay was pretty, probably a year or two older, and had the speech and bearing of someone who had attended the best schools and expected the best of the world. Like many of the kids he had gone to college with. The coke, or whatever it was, surprised him, as did the cigarette. But then in her class of people there were always rebels, those who made a mission of subverting expectations. A friend of his from the canoe club was a Northrop—a Northrop Grumman Northrop—and had graduated two years before and gone to northern Michigan and become a cop. He wanted to ask her about the anchor, but instead he said, "Sir Will doesn't fish. Doesn't seem to. What's he doing here?"

Shay crushed her cigarette against the log wall and squatted. From behind a potted lavender by the door she took a Ziploc bag and dropped her butt in with a bunch of others and tucked the bag back in its hiding place. She winced a smile. "Kurt has a nose on him. Okay, cowboy, it's been fun," she said, and turned.

Jack put a hand on her arm and he felt it tense under her blouse. It was not soft, she was very strong. He wanted to ask her about that, too: she was not much older but he'd bet she had worked ranches, or maybe boats—the kind of sailing yachts that had manual winches where the crew had to be super fit. But now she froze and he knew the moment could tilt in either direction. "Um," he said. "I was wondering what those twenty-odd breakfasts were for."

Her face was two feet away. She had always seemed game and fun. She always brought a gust of ebullient energy to the table whenever she came around with wine or a new course. Jack understood why Jensen, who seemed to know everything, would cut her a little slack when it came to a cigarette now and then. But now her eyes were sad, and he saw fear there, too.

"Can't say," she said.

"Can't because you'd lose your job?"

Her eyes searched his. There was not the defiance in them he expected; instead it seemed she was looking for a place to land her boat, or anchor.

"NDA," she said. She saw his puzzlement. "Oh yeah, you're a cowboy. Nondisclosure agreement."

His hand was still around her biceps. "Well, I need to know."

"Well, tough."

"Well, how about I mention to Kurt that you're doing blow behind the kitchen?"

Her expression hardened. "Go ahead."

"And then while you were jacked up you started spilling info on the guests. Like full names and who gets plastered."

Jack saw the fear flash across her eyes again. There and gone, like a coyote running in shade at the edge of the trees.

"You're not a snitch. I've been watching you."

"I need to know," Jack said. "It's gone past polite."

She sucked in a deep breath and yanked her arm from his grasp. "I know you probably live on a horse. But out on the range or wherever, you ever hear of celebrity rehabs?" Yep, they'd gone past polite. Jack didn't say anything. "Well, they always end up in BuzzFeed or *TMZ*, you know those shots of the poor things in big sunglasses and T-shirts, hair all wild, trying to hide their faces as they exit some treatment center?" Now he nodded. "Well, there's no paparazzi here. And these aren't just hapless celebrities."

Jack was trying to digest it. He said, "Will and . . . Neave, they don't fish, but . . . they stay here, get treatment. The others at Kreutzer's . . ." He trailed off. He was trying to fit puzzle pieces together. "But some do fish, like Alison . . ."

"Think about it, cowboy," she said. Jack grimaced. "If the CEO of a major corporation is spinning out of control, needs to get clean, but if the board or whatever finds out, it's splitsville, walk the plank, dude—well, where does the dude go?"

Jack was no longer looking at her. He wasn't seeing the night anymore, either, his imagination and memory were traveling . . . what added up?

Now it was she squeezing his arm. "If you mention one word, I lose my job that fast. Not kidding. *And* get sued. I mean it. I like you, I do, but you just put me out on the thinnest ice and I'm not sure I appreciate it." She spun around, swept the stainless pot off the ground, and shoved back into the kitchen.

•

On his way back up the road, a shadow stepped out from the trail to the pool house. A big shadow. Kurt. Jack could just see his face in the porch lights from the lodge. He was not happy.

"Thought I told you we discourage guides and guests from going into town."

Jack stepped back. Instinct. He never let himself get into a grapple.

"How'd you know we went into town?"

Kurt didn't say anything. He turned his head and spat. "You're getting out on thinner ice," he said.

"Second time I've heard that tonight. Why? 'Cause I felt like drinking something different than Cutthroat ale?"

"You make trouble, don't you?" the manager said quietly. "Wherever you go." He turned and walked back up into the shadows toward the main house.

That stung. That might be true, Jack thought.

•

That night Jack lay awake on the bed fully dressed except boots, with the Pendleton blanket pulled over him and his hands folded under his head. No reason he could articulate, except that he couldn't sleep and somehow undressing, getting into sheets, slipping off, even, into sleep, would make him more vulnerable than he wanted to be right now. It had been a long day—of fishing, of being closer to Alison, of new people who were smart and challenging—of revelation. Was it? Revelation in Shay's explanation?

He didn't know. It wasn't just Kurt. Something was off, as it had been at this place from the first moment he was shown his quarters. Even his vulnerability: he sensed danger, but he wasn't at all sure why, or from where. He might be suffering from PTSD after all—what Wynn's mother had gently suggested on the phone when he had called to check in last winter.

He wished he could talk to Pop. As reticent as his father could be, he was as clear-eyed a person as he had ever known, and had sound judgment to go along with it. Uncle Lloyd, too. Lloyd was an extravagant storyteller, and as much as he moved within a cloud of his own laughter, he shared with his brother that remarkable ability to see things clearly and to act with prudence and courage. Jack wished he could be like them. Maybe it was what he wished for more than anything, except for being able to do two days in his life over again.

It must have been a few hours before dawn when he drifted to sleep. The alarm on his iPhone went off and he shunted the blasts of the hunting horns into his dream, where he was on some kind of warship that had been rocked by an explosion and the bulkheads were gushing seawater and the PA speakers were blaring the all-hands siren. He woke with gray light in the windows and his heart racing and some kind of grief from the dream and he realized as he remembered the last images that there were no other crew in the gangways, no shouts or running sailors. It tore him—the utter solitude of the disaster. And as he sat up against the headboard he thought, or felt, that dying among a band of brothers, or within one's tribe, was better than trying to get to a lifeboat alone.

He turned off the alarm, left the phone on the bed table, rubbed his eyes. How different we were than wild animals, or even house cats. They'd had one cat at the ranch they let in the house, and she slept on his legs or feet every night of his life until midway through high school, when she died. When she died she did not find her way to his bed, where he would have lifted her to her usual spot, but she vanished, and he found her a day later curled up in the dust behind the furnace off the laundry room. People need people, more than any other being needs any other being, and Jack thought as he sifted the remnants of the nightmare that the need makes us particularly vulnerable.

Well, he needed coffee. Maybe company, too. He would have loved the reassurance of Alison beside him in the night, but she was not at all clingy and she knew how to give a new friendship room to breathe. Was it a friendship? He didn't know what it was. No need to label it. In the taxonomies of relationships there were plenty of strange outliers and hybrids.

He reached for the phone without looking and heard the thunk as it fell to the floor. Damn. Lucky it had a silicone case. Stiffly, as if he'd taken a long hike the day before, he eased out of bed and crouched into a crawl to look for his phone. Dim in the cabin and he didn't see it, but he felt under the bedstead, which was a wooden box with maybe an inch gap above the floorboards. He could just get his fingers underneath it to swipe along its length. He did and hit the side of his phone, good, and pulled it out. Except it wasn't his phone.

•

It was green. A green case with a pale pink stripe down the middle and the black spot pattern of a rainbow trout. Jack understood immediately that the phone was Ken's. Now he was wide awake. It was an iPhone and, still on hands and knees, he touched the screen and it lit. Of course it did. Probably only four days since . . . he wouldn't let his mind go there. Jack swiped the phone. It was not password protected. It opened on the voice memo app. There were two new recordings. One was titled "URGENT To the Next Guy." The latest one said simply, "FUCKED."

Jack tapped the first. The voice was young, breathless as if the boy had just been running. It was energized with near panic. "You're the next guy. Prolly a guide. Some shit going on here, I don't even know. Had a evening off, scouting elk for bow season, nothing says we can't hunt . . . I saw the kids—"

The voice cut. Jack was on all fours and for a second he couldn't breathe. He remembered the girl running down the road, the deputy intercepting her and slamming her against the car hood. Her terror-stricken face, the scratches on it.

He breathed. He hit the next memo, "FUCKED." "Okay I'm fucked I think. If you're listening I am, I really am." Now the kid sounded beyond panic. "One of the mercs saw me. Sure of it. I told Jensen there was family trouble and I need out, sorry. Looked at me like I was a worm, said I was broken. Cuz of the . . . getting caught selling. Fuck him. That was a year ago, I was just helping Sean. Jensen said Den only hires broken people. Said nobody believes 'em. Fuck 'em all. Going back up for one more look and then I'm gone." Kid had more nerve than Jack had figured. He was clearly scared and pissed off at once. "Den is watching everything. Check the thermostat" was the last thing he said. Then the memo cut.

•

Broken people. Nobody believes 'em. Us.

The heat was in Jack's face. On his knees on the rag rug he was actually shaking. It was a blind fury. Is that the way they—Den, Kurt, whoever—saw him?

He moved his fingers up toward the head of the bed and felt his own phone and retrieved it. He AirDropped the two voice memos to himself and slid Ken's phone back under the bed. He stood slowly, glanced at the Nest thermostat on the east wall, and couldn't think of what to do except walk over to it. It was round and black with a digital screen in the center that said OFF. He ran his fingers around the cover and with a sharp pull he popped it off. And saw, stuck to a small circuit board, the camera lens. No bigger than the one on his phone, and unmistakable.

It faced the bed, took in the whole small room, porch door to headboard. If he felt angry and violated before, when he found the camera that watched him fish under the bridge, now it was a white rage. He was about to yank out the bead of lens, but stopped. He took a deep breath and swiftly replaced the cover and tapped the thermostat to ON, and ran his finger up the screen until the digital number said 70. Anyone watching through the camera would only see a man who had slept in his clothes, probably too cold with just the blankets; see him approach the thermostat and deliberate and turn it on. And they would think that this tough young honcho guide was really a wimp after all.

CHAPTER EIGHT

Only now did he strip off yesterday's clothes and take a hot shower in the narrow stall, letting the scalding water pound his neck and shoulders. Eyes closed, he found the razor he'd propped on the soap shelf, and he shaved himself by feel, and by feel nicked his left ear, damn, and washed his hair with the miniature shampoo someone—who was it? Ana—had left a few days before. How many days? It already seemed like a lifetime . . .

The whole shower might have taken five minutes. When he dried himself there was blood on the white towel. The nick on the ridge just above his earlobe must have held some kind of blood vessel because it always took too long to stop bleeding and if he was going to cut himself anywhere, he unerringly found it. He tore off a corner of TP and pressed it onto the cut and it adhered itself and flowered with crimson. In his zip toilet kit he found the vial of styptic powder and he peeled off the sopped tissue and dabbed the cut and it miraculously stopped. Good.

He had two pairs of clean jeans in the dresser and he pulled one on, and a clean camo tech fishing shirt, and hiking boots not shitkickers, and he coasted the bike down to the lodge.

•

He stood outside with the bike and he made himself look up as if he were admiring the last stars in a luminous sea of blue. The cold and heedless distances always calmed him, and did now. Cooled the fury, a little.

Okay, he murmured, *act like a guide.*

Before he entered he saw the new couple's rods already strung in the rack on the outside wall. Curious, he stepped over. They were Winston five weights like his and he lifted them up lightly and turned them toward the porch light. He examined the blanks just forward of the cork grips where he knew the company always engraved the name: *Y. Takagi* on one, *T. Takagi* on the other.

Alison was at the fire already, as were Yumi and Teiji, and he was happy to see them in conversation, he wasn't sure why. The bona fide Knight Commander of the British Empire and his mute wife wore brightly patterned Norwegian sweaters this morning, and were already seated at their usual table, which was odd. It was as if they wished to remain securely apart this morning. They nodded at Jack and he noticed that the brightness had returned to their eyes and that they were animated. Sir Will had a pair of compact binoculars and he trained them out the window, handed them to Neave. Jack fetched his coffee and as he approached and greeted everyone good morning

Alison studied him a moment too long, and her eyes flickered with concern. He wondered if he was so obviously upset.

The new couple was dressed head to toe in quick-dry khaki. They bowed from the neck and raised their cups—osprey for him, kingfisher for her. Jack appreciated the Takagis. He thought, how perfect: the husband chose a bird of prey as did she. Both birds were fishers but each had different strategies, and he thought that on the river they probably fished with different tactics and style. It would allow them, statistically, to show the trout more and different targets, but he bet that it also contributed to a more harmonious time on the river, which Jack thought fit their personalities.

Alison said her usual "Sleep well?" and Jack said, "Yes, thank you." Which was true for a couple of hours. And he could see that she knew he was lying.

That's when Jack asked whom the couple would be fishing with and they glanced at each other and Teiji said, "No one. We prefer to be led to the water like a horse . . ." Teiji interrupted himself. He was smart enough, Jack thought, to see that his metaphor might lead to the perception of an insult to this guide, which Teiji did not at all want to convey. But Jack appreciated it. Being led to the water and forced to drink put being guided in a whole new light.

Jack rescued him. "I get it. It's good to fish new water and use the skills you've learned on similar streams to figure it out. And sometimes the solitude is the best part."

Yumi nodded; it was more like a bow. "That is well put, thank you. That is what we enjoy best." And she turned to Alison, not wanting to disrespect her, either, in any way. "And we also often still find employing a guide to be the most productive and fun."

God, Jack thought. There you have it: it is the most fun either way. Amazing. Was there anyone more polite on earth? Or thoughtful? Did it take twice as much energy to go through the world being this considerate? Alison smiled. She, too, appreciated the effort. She said, "I just go with Jack because he's cute and tells killer stories." Which was pretty much true. Scary stories. Jack saw Yumi blush.

"Has anyone oriented you at all?" he said to the Takagis. "The boundaries, the bridge, the trail?"

"Yes, thank you," Teiji said. "Mr. Jensen gave us a very good description from the deck. We plan to fish from just below the bridge upstream this morning. That is, if it does not interfere with the two of you. And then we will have massage and spa treatment in the afternoon."

"Yes," Yumi chimed. "We have been working terribly hard at home. We plan to fish half the time."

"And relax the other half," Alison said. "That sounds perfect to me."

Perfect, Jack thought. Fishing and spa time. Or, if Shay was telling the truth, some kind of addiction treatment? The Takagis were the least addicted-seeming people he had ever met. Maybe they would just get massages. But what about Ken, what he had said on the memo, what he had seen. Kids? Half-naked like the girl on the road? Was all this a front for some kind of sex-trafficking ring? He had to remind himself again that he wasn't the best judge of people, but the Takagis did not seem that type, either. God. He was saved by the bell, because just then Shay breezed out from the kitchen and rang it.

•

The Takagis were thoughtful enough to allow the famous singer and her guide to have breakfast to themselves. It was clear to Jack that they knew who she was, he could see it in the deference with which they spoke to her, see it in Yumi's almost painful shyness. But of course they would never raise that part of her life in conversation and Jack could see that they expected the same discretion. And just because they had been invited to join Alison for dinner, they in no way assumed that there was an open invitation for breakfast. They made it clear by their demeanor that they very much enjoyed the company, and also that they would never take anything that wasn't offered. There was nothing at all sticky about them, nor were they aloof. Jack marveled. He wondered what it would be like to move through life with that much assurance and composure.

So he and Alison seated themselves at their table by the window, looking down on the first direct sunlight pouring into the canyon like a tide. And they saw below two ducks wing past, the pair in perfect tandem, arrowing downstream—a stuttered flash of white and teal not fifteen feet off the water. *What could be better?* Again: if one could focus on a tiny corner of the cosmos. Shay said, "Beautiful morning," and poured more coffee and used tongs to coax fresh hot croissants out of a cloth-covered basket. "There's local honey in that little ceramic pot," she said, and wouldn't look at Jack.

When she was gone, Alison leaned forward. It *was* a beautiful morning, and warm, and she herself was stunning. She was wearing a black sports bra and a light cotton button-down open to the sternum. When she leaned forward the table swelled the tops of her freckled breasts and he felt a stab of desire. Could a person be swept by so many emotions at once? The last half hour had been pretty damn rich.

"What's up with you and Miss Shay?" she said. "She won't look at you. Did you call her mother a name?"

"Sort of."

"And you look a little cross-eyed."

"I am."

"Wanna tell me?"

"I think so. But not here."

She raised one russet eyebrow and winked at him. He thought she did, it was so fast. And she said, "More will be revealed." When she said it, he couldn't help but think of her taking off her clothes. He checked himself with an unspoken *Get your shit together* . . .

That was the way the morning was going. He looked out to the deck expecting to see Cody and the Youngens breakfasting by their usual fire, but the table was empty.

CHAPTER NINE

They dropped to the river but didn't fish. They sat on a log in the deep shade. Through the trees they saw the Takagis come down the steep railroad-tie steps and hit the river trail and turn upstream. Someone was doing what they said they would do.

It was nice to sit and listen to the stream in conversation with itself. It chortled and lapped and threshed. Jack could see an ouzel hopping rock to rock at water's edge, diving into a burbling pocket and jumping out. The little black bird glistened like the wet stones, and seemed rounded by water like the cobbles, and it bobbed where it stood with its signature inborn rhythm.

They weren't in any rush. He needed the calm of the bird, of the morning. As if reading his mind, Alison said, "I wanna go really slow this morning."

"Me, too," he said.

"If we fish one seam all morning, that's okay with me."

"Okay."

He needed the time anyway, to get his thoughts together. They wheeled like a kaleidoscope, without the symmetries. He and Alison sat in silence, both content for the moment just to listen to the babblings of the river, and birdsong, to hear the canyon waking into its day. Alison touched Jack's arm. "Look," she whispered. He looked. Coming down the steps at a run was . . . Cody. Jack didn't imagine a kid like that running, ever, unless he was on a horse. But he was athletic and balanced, even in his packer boots, and he hit the river trail yards from where they sat, and turned upstream at a brisk trot, just in front of them, through the scrim of trees. A few minutes later he was coming back, this time leading the Takagis. Jack and Alison went very still. The little group was twenty feet away and they could hear them clearly, Teiji saying, "We are embarrassed."

"It happens," Cody was saying over his shoulder.

Teiji: "We are so sorry. We were certain the treatments were in the afternoon."

Yumi (carrying her rod as any expert through trees and over rough ground—by the reel, with the length of the rod facing backward where it would not double and break in a fall, or snag on a branch): "Yes, we were certain it was afternoon."

Cody: "That's tomorrow. No harm, no foul, they're just getting started."

They passed in single file, briskly, and went up the steps.

Alison chuckled softly. "They take their massage appointments pretty seriously around here."

They're just getting started. Jack shook his head. That didn't sound like a massage and spa, that sounded like addiction therapy, AA group, whatever. But, as he thought at breakfast, the Takagis were—seemed—the antithesis of addicts. The only excess they seemed to indulge in was politeness.

"What?" Alison said. "You look really disturbed now." She poked him. "Are you wishing *you* were getting a massage?"

Jack started as if just waking, as if just realizing she was beside him.

"Sorry," he said. "I had an interesting talk with Shay last night. And . . . other things."

"I was thinking that," she said.

He told her. About the conversation outside the kitchen door. About the nondisclosure agreement, the treatment center disguised as a neighbor.

"For the mega-rich and famous apparently," he said.

"I never heard of it. What am I, chopped liver?"

"You're not desperate and strung out."

"When you fish with me in the mountains of North Carolina I might tell you that story."

"I'd like that."

"You're supposed to be telling me stories now. Remember, I told the Young and the Guideless that that's why I employed you."

"You hinted at another reason and Yumi blushed hard."

"Tell me more about Shay."

"Well, she said the rehab or whatever is super secret and it's the only reason the folks who come here don't get plastered all over BuzzFeed. She said that if you're someone like a big CEO with a drug problem and the board of the company can't know, you come here."

"Okaay . . ."

"Well, that suddenly made a lot of sense. The security, the not wanting anyone to have guns, Will and Neave looking so drugged out. I thought maybe the IV marks on the back of their hands—his hand—were from some high-powered Antabuse, but . . ." He trailed off.

"What?"

"They were all drinking mojitos the other night."

"Maybe theirs were virgin. We weren't there when they ordered."

"Yeah, that occurred to me. But then I was thinking about us getting shot at. And the wading boot I saw half-buried and how when I went back it was gone. What Shay said, it—" He stopped. He was still trying to grapple with everything he had witnessed.

"What?"

"It made some sense. It explained a lot. Not all. I was thinking maybe eighty percent. It was the other twenty percent that really bothered me."

"So?"

"So this morning I found an iPhone under my bed."

•

There was no way to tell it except to tell it. What his father always said.

So he told her. About Ken's message. How he, Jack, was certain it was Ken's boot he had seen in the spruce. The almost panicked urgency of the two voice memos, the one saying he had been scouting elk and something about kids, the other saying he was sure he had been seen by a "merc," and he was now certain he was fucked. How he told Jensen he was quitting and Kurt had said Den only hires broken people because nobody believes them. How Den watches everything and how Ken had said to check the thermostat.

"Did you?" Alison said. She had the look of a child trying to make sense of an awful Grimms' fairy tale for the first time. "Did you check it?"

"Sure."

"And?"

"There was a frigging camera in there. Pointed right at my bed. Taking in the whole room."

"No way. What'd you do?"

"I turned on the thermostat. So it looked like that's why I was messing with it."

"Good thinking," she said. But her tone was not at all sure.

•

"Wanna fish?" Jack said. "It's about all we can do right now."

"Okay," she said. "Sure. Yes, yes, I want to. Let's think about something else. Jeez."

They fished. Slowly. Neither was very enthused at the start, but Jack was such a natural, his choices and motions so ingrained, and she had so much poise—in her movements and patience—that they caught fish. When the top fly hitched and she set the hook and the rod bent and quivered—that connection, with another being, with a life force erased for the moment all other considerations. It demanded full attention, which is its own version of joy. For a couple of hours they moved in the cold current, and the river granted them a measure of her heedless grace.

At noon, a half hour before lunch, they packed it in. They climbed the trail to Jack's cabin and continued down the sandy road toward the lodge and lunch. Alison said, "Hey, let's swing up to the pool house on the way. I think I'll knock off early this afternoon and take a sauna. Lord knows I don't think I can sweat out the creeps, but it'd feel good."

So they turned up the path into the aspen grove above the pond where the pool lay in its own log sanctuary surrounded by glass garage doors, all open now to the breezy afternoon. They walked unspeaking side by side and Jack stopped and put his hand on her arm. He pulled her back behind two twin trees. He pointed up the hill to where Shay's cart track ran and they saw a golf cart bumping down it slowly. This cart had a back bench seat, not a cargo bed, and on the seat, holding to the vertical pipes that supported the roof, were Yumi and Teiji. They were coming from upcanyon, from the main house and parking lot, or beyond. Was it Kreutzer's? The thought sent a frisson of panic through Jack, like the jolt of dissonance in a nightmare when nothing was adding up. They were supposed to be having massages or whatever, weren't they? But more shocking were their faces. They were maybe thirty yards off and Jack and Alison could see them clearly. Yumi was sheet white, her face rigid, and against this mask the tears ran. Teiji sat erect, his expression stoic, eyes straight ahead, and though he was sitting shoulder to shoulder with his wife he looked terribly alone.

They jostled past. Somebody Jack did not recognize drove them, a young clean-cut guy in a red polo shirt.

"What the heck?" Alison whispered. "Did you see their faces?"

"Uh huh. I feel queasy."

"Me, too. God. Didn't look like they just came from relaxing bodywork."

"Let's go down," Jack said. "Can you invite them to our table?"

"Yeah, sure. I might not eat much."

•

They stripped waders on the porch, hung them on the pegs, pulled on the running shoes they had left there. She put up her rod, and they located their table on the deck. Full house today, the other couples were already there. The vibe was friendly, if a little forced. Will and Neave and the Youngens were at their own tables and seemed in a haze of distraction, but they made an effort to smile, lift a hand. Stiff smiles maybe, but smiles. Everybody, it seemed, was acting. Except the Takagis. They were about to sit down at the only table left, in the sun in the middle of the deck, when Alison stepped over and asked if they cared to join her. The Takagis were startled. As was Alison when she saw their faces. They seemed suddenly years older, as if they'd just been through a natural disaster or lost a child. The poise was gone. Teiji hesitated. Alison gestured at her table, which was the farthest table downstream. It was in the shade, and against the railing overlooking the river, and much more secluded than being in the center of the patio. Maybe it tipped the decision, because Yumi said,

"Yes. Yes, thank you. We will." And she seemed relieved.

The four sat and gratefully downed a full tumbler each of sweetened iced tea. Yumi blinked as she drank and would not look past her glass. Shay put down a basket of hot homemade potato chips and again wouldn't look at Jack. Teiji ordered a Sapporo beer. Comfort in the familiar. Yumi called Shay back and asked for a hot sake. Teiji forced himself to ask how the fishing went. His eyes were red, as if he'd been crying, or wanted to.

"It was decent," Alison said. "We didn't slay them, but we made a solid effort. You?"

"We didn't fish. Our treatments were this morning," Yumi said. "We made a mistake."

Well, she didn't say "spa treatments." At least she was not lying.

"Was it nice?" Alison said.

"It was . . ." A smile fluttered to her lips and trembled there. Jack thought she was trying her hardest not to weep. He also noticed that she held the tumbler with her left hand, and her right was under the table. As was Teiji's. Who interjected,

"It was not what we expected."

"I'm sorry," Alison said.

Shay brought the beer and sake on a tray. She set the heavier Sapporo down first, followed by the glass, which she filled. The hot sake was in a small hand-glazed porcelain bottle painted with flying cranes. Shay lifted it from the tray and Yumi reached up with both hands to take it and Jack noticed the Band-Aid on the back of her right hand.

"Thank you," Yumi said. And then Jack saw her turn the bottle to see the design and her face startled again, and tightened. She handed it back to Shay. "Can you please put it in another vessel," she said. "Do you have one with carp?"

Shay cocked her head as if mishearing, but immediately recovered her aplomb. "Of course. Yes, I think we do."

Teiji rescued his wife again. "Cranes can be a symbol of death," he said.

"Oh!" Alison said. "I had no idea."

"Thank you," Yumi said, bowing her head. For what, Jack wasn't sure. A general sympathy, he guessed.

"Well, whew," Alison said. "Well, at least we can all fish this afternoon. We can work around whatever section you want to try."

Finally Yumi lifted her head and met Alison's eye. "Actually, we are leaving."

"Leaving?"

"Yes. We asked the lodge to book us on the late-afternoon flight from Gunnison."

"Oh." Jack had not seen Alison at a loss, but now she was. "May I ask why?" she said.

"We are not at all happy with the scheduling," she said.

"The service is not what we expected," Teiji said.

No shit, Jack thought. And just as he thought it he heard the thud of a boot on the deck and turned to see Kurt Jensen making his way straight to their table.

•

The manager tipped his hat to Alison and the Takagis, who looked away. Jack thought that was odd. If anything governed their behavior it was unwavering graciousness, which even now, as shaken as they seemed to be, they were attempting to display. Had been until this moment. Kurt towered over Jack and said quietly enough that the other tables couldn't hear, "No lunch today. No time. Let's have a chat." Kurt lifted his chin toward the porch steps.

"What?" Jack put down the basket he'd just picked up.

"Let's go around front," Kurt said.

"Excuse me?" Alison said, loud enough for everyone. But Kurt was already moving and Jack followed. So did Alison. When the three got to the fishing rod rack at the corner of the front porch, out of earshot of the lunch tables, the manager turned. He straightened himself when he saw Alison K.

"I'm sorry, ma'am," he said. "I truly am. It's a company matter."

"Was there something so momentous you wanted to tell my guide? That he couldn't eat his lunch after a long morning of fishing?"

Kurt didn't meet her eyes. He studied the grass at his feet as if coming to a decision and then he looked straight at her. "Your guide," he said. "I'm gonna have to let him go." He turned to Jack. "You're fired."

Alison stiffened. "Can I ask you why?" she said, very low.

"Best not to go into details," Kurt said.

"Let's go into details, why don't we?" she said. Her voice was the tool of her trade and it carried. Jack held his breath. There was still a steel gate and a long empty road between them and anywhere safe. Maybe half a county to get across. He tried to catch her eye but in her fury she had only one target.

Jensen swung around and in his face Jack could see the surprise and also the steel of an old horse trainer. A problem horse that acted up just when you wanted to get lunch was part of the job.

"It's done," he said, without his usual deference to guests. "I'm sorry."

"I don't think so," she said. If he was steeled, her blood was up. Her eyes were a flashing true green, and she was flushed but assured. She seemed to Jack like a seasoned warrior about to do what she was trained to do. "He's the best goddamned guide I've ever had, and I'm here for five more days."

"I don't doubt it," Kurt said. "Him being extra good. And I know you two have a special relationship, but—"

"Are you being rude now, Mr. Jensen?" she flared. "Is this what the Kingfisher Lodge gets you for twenty grand a week?"

Jensen, Jack saw, was throttled. His mouth opened, and he closed it. Whatever else he was, he'd been a rancher first, born and bred, as Jack was, and he had an inborn code of civility and tact which he knew he had just violated. It may have mortified him, but Jack doubted it. He clearly had bigger things on his plate.

She did not wait for him to get his footing. "Like I said," she seethed. "Let's talk about details. How would it go over if I announced to my one-point-one-million Twitter followers that I came to the Kingfisher Lodge and got shot at, and treated to snide sexual comments by the rudest manager, and that the personnel situation was chaotic, and that local fishermen were getting mauled nearly to death by out-of-control neighbor dogs? That all sounds like a country song, doesn't it?"

He opened his mouth again. Jack thought he looked like a fish gawping for oxygen.

"Well," Kurt stammered. Jack never thought he'd see the man at a loss. "Uh . . ."

Jack said, "Mr. Jensen, can I ask you why you're letting me go?" He didn't give a shit, he just wanted to hear what Kurt would say.

The big man turned. His neck was red. He said, "I asked you to bring up your firearms and you didn't. At this place, with this clientele, that's a serious breach. I told you that. I waited. I gave you three days' grace and that grace is up."

"I'll bring it up to the office now," Jack said. "Right after lunch."

"It's the attitude more than anything," Kurt said. Jack could tell he was trying to keep himself from snarling. "Truth be told."

"Just what I'm thinking," Alison shot back. "Your attitude, Mr. Jensen. Let's tell the world all about it."

Kurt stood on the little patch of mowed grass. He looked from Jack to Alison K and back. Jack knew the manager was weighing every consequence and Jack also knew that the reasons he'd given for dismissal were bullshit. Which rang alarm bells. How much did the man know? Of Jack's nocturnal activities, of his other little hikes? Of hers? Someone had smoothed over the duff under the spruce, that was bad enough. Jack really did want to pack up his shit right now and climb in his truck and leave, but there was no way he was going to leave her, and he was not going to leave the terror-stricken girl he'd seen on the road if that was part of the "kids" Ken had mentioned in the recording.

Was it a trafficking ring? That's what occurred to him. Sex trafficking for billionaires while they got treatment for their other addictions? Was that what had shaken the Takagis? Jack stood in the sun and blinked at his boss and thought, *I am already dead.* And what he meant was that when his mother died he did, too, partially; and a lot of the rest of him went with Wynn. There wasn't a whole lot to lose here.

"I will," he said again. "I'm really sorry, Mr. Jensen. I'll bring the rifle up now."

Jensen's mouth was set and he looked from one to the other. Then he shook his head in disgust and turned on his heel and walked back up the track.

•

One thing with rich and famous people: discretion is a currency. They grant it and expect it in return, and so when Alison and Jack walked across the open back porch the other couples only gave the briefest of glances, quick smiles, and went back to their lunches. But the Takagis were gone.

They ate in silence, mostly, each in their own thoughts. After a strawberry-rhubarb cobbler in heavy cream, and coffee, they nodded to the other couples and walked off the deck and unhooked their waders from the pegs on the front porch. That's when Jack felt in the chest pocket and his iPhone was gone.

CHAPTER TEN

They both needed a break. He rolled up his waders and tucked them under his arm. He didn't say anything to her. Stuff was mounting up, the sense of threat. As much as he needed an ally, there was nothing they could do now about the phone and there was no point in adding to her burden.

She wanted to swim in the pool and take a sauna and relax, and he badly wanted to just sit in the cane rocker on his little cabin porch and let everything sift. Read a chapter of his latest Murakami novel, or Li Xue's poems from *The Orchard*. They would reconvene at 3:30 and fish the late afternoon until dinner.

But first he had to play ball. Play ball with Kurt and the lodge enough to get through the next few days. Jensen already wanted to stomp him into jelly, Jack could see it in his eyes plain as day. Fair enough, the feeling was now mutual. Was it Wednesday? He checked his watch. Yes. Alison was scheduled to leave after fishing Monday morning. If he could just maintain. If they could. Fish and share meals and keep their cool and get her out of here. He could do the rest, whatever it was. The lodge knew he knew something, but not what, he was certain. They were worried, but not sure, which is why they were just trying to get him off the property. *Den hires people no one would believe . . .* Otherwise he, too, would be half buried by now, like Ken the Hen, right where he tried to flee.

Ken had been dispatched hurriedly, Jack was sure. Probably right where he had been apprehended after seeing whatever he had seen—running down the creek, down the only route he knew well. Because he was just a fishing guide like Jack, who could read a river but was maybe not so good at reading men. And Jack bet it had happened just the night before he had arrived, and they'd covered Ken fast in the spruce duff against the smell, and had meant to deal with him properly on Jack's first night but something had come up. It was Alison! He remembered now how she had said that she truly liked to walk in the middle of the night and listen and look for night birds, and had done so on her first night there. She had probably almost walked right into them.

He thought of the Takagis. They had not been in the spa house or the massage cabin; they had been coming from upstream and they did not look at all happy.

He walked back up to his cabin slowly. *Play ball.* He'd go retrieve his .30-.30 from behind the tree where he'd hidden it and bring it up now to the main house and let them lock it in the safe or whatever. He put on baggy shorts and a T-shirt and found his flip-flops in a side pocket of his duffel bag and wriggled his feet into them. It was the first really hot afternoon and he might as well go casual. Look relaxed. Look the opposite of a guy who had just decided he had hardly anything to lose.

CHAPTER ELEVEN

The rifle was leaning against the tree where he left it, so he slung it over his back and walked up through patches of shade to the main house. A late August afternoon in the mountains, hot in the sun and where the trees threw their shadows it was almost chilly. He loved this, this time of year. When he wasn't guiding he wet-waded in just shorts and let the cold shaded bends raise goose bumps and then he'd round a corner into full sun and the sudden heat would smooth them out. He liked getting back to his truck and pulling on a sweater as the sun went over the ridge. Within a month the aspen would be turning and spreading gold down the shoulders of the ridges and up high there might be a flurry of first snow.

The way things ought to be. A turning of seasons and a natural acceptance of life pulling back and many things passing. There was a kind of relief in that, and a sharp beauty. Whose power had much to do with one's ability to hold the losses it augured.

That's what he thought as his flip-flops crunched the dry needles fallen in the track. That there was something unnatural going on here. He wasn't sure what it was, but he could feel it, as strongly as he could feel the wind that blew upstream at sundown. People here were trying to subvert the natural order somehow and it was twisting the energies of the place into a vortex where the pressure dropped.

When he was at college he took a course on *Moby-Dick* from Marilynne Robinson, the great novelist and scholar. She must have been eighty, but still vigorous, and she had the light in her eye of someone who has been looking for the truest things every minute of her life. She liked him for some reason—Jack thought that maybe she had never taught a kid from rural Colorado who had read more on his own than most of the other students—and she invited him for tea at her house across the river. It was a small yellow-painted clapboard on the far side of a Vermont village whose main street was the county road that wound over the shoulder of a wooded mountain to the next town. They sat in metal spring rockers in the garden under a hummingbird feeder, and they ended up talking about the warming that was devastating the forests in Jack's valley at home. And Jack rocked forward and squeezed his glass and said, "What is evil? What do you think it is?"

She didn't think more than a second. She tossed her loose gray hair off the side of her face and said, "Impediment to Being."

That simple. Jack had thought about it ever since.

He stepped up onto the porch and turned to survey the grounds. From here he could see five of the cabins set into the trees, dappled in afternoon sunlight, and a corner of the lodge below, and the parking area to his right. Beautiful layout. Glorious, really.

He saw a golf cart bumping up the sandy road. It was Ana, the short housekeeper, shuttling a stack of folded towels and sheets from somewhere to somewhere. She glanced toward the office as she passed and recognized him and her face lit with a smile. She waved and he waved back. *Tres, tres, nueve, tres*, he thought and shrugged. Then he went through the screen door of the office cabin.

A woman he'd never seen before was behind the pine counter. She was maybe twenty-eight, athletic, with the stylish blond bob and reflexive bright smile of a real estate agent. How Jack thought of her, anyway. She wore a periwinkle linen shirt and a black Voormi wool vest, and when her smile had relaxed enough to allow speech she said, "Jack, hi. Kelly. Brr, it looks hot, but it's actually chilly out of the sun."

"What I was just thinking."

"I see you brought me something. Good."

"Yep, seems to have caused a lot of brain damage. Apologies."

"Well."

The smile turned on again. "A place like this doesn't run without clear rules."

Jack didn't say anything. "Clear" is one way of putting it, he thought. "Here," he said. He unslung the carbine, held the barrel to the floor, jacked the lever, and put a finger in the breach to double check that it wasn't loaded and eased down the hammer with his thumb. Still aiming at the varnished planks, he pulled the trigger for a dry fire to take the pressure off the spring and laid it on the counter.

"Would you like a receipt?" she said.

"Yes, ma'am."

"Okay, just a sec. I'll just put this in the closet."

She took a key out of a drawer and walked into the next room, which served as a fly shop and swag store and, apparently, as an armory. Kelly, he thought. Someone like her, does she know? Whatever there is to know?

On the counter was a teak business card holder. Her card said "Kelly Koplinger, Guest Services and Marketing." He knew people like her, or thought he did. She operated in a simple universe of gain and loss, cause and effect, pleasure and pain. Or wanted to. If you ran ten kilometers, you maintained your fitness level, and if you pushed yourself and made better time than the day before you could add a tick to the plus column. If you signed up ten guests, your fifteen percent commission would be so much, and would put your August earnings up twelve percent year over year. Like that. The birds you saw on your run or what went on behind the closed doors of the lodge never dented your consciousness because you had erected an impermeable membrane, in order to keep a clean focus on the things that mattered.

He knew when he thought like this he was being terribly judgmental and probably sophomoric. Because nobody was simple. Nobody on earth. The four chambers of the heart and all the crenellations in the human brain made certain of it. And it was pain that drove a desire for a simple calculus, and pain was infinitely manifold. He also knew that in the gaps between all those firing neurons was plenty of space for the divine and nobody, really, could protect against it.

Hell, maybe she was an expert bird watcher. Maybe she practiced the viola every evening. He had a hard time imagining Kelly sleeping so well at night knowing trafficking or murder was a part of the business plan of the place she worked.

He also saw just over the counter, on the high desk behind it, a black telephone in its cradle. Jack stepped out onto the porch to wait. He looked through the aspen to the little parking area and front gate and saw Cody walk to his truck and climb in. Jack shuddered and looked away.

•

On his own porch he tried to read. This was the porch he had seen just a few days ago and thought, *I could sit here for the rest of my life and watch the river.* How much could change in a few days. He sat in one of the rockers and put the book in his lap. It was *The Orchard: Poems of Li Xue,* one of his favorite collections of poetry. It was by a poet of eighth-century China who had gone into self-exile with her daughter and written some of the most exquisite poems of the T'ang Dynasty. She was an aficionado of loss and also of nature, which Jack could relate to right now. He closed his eyes and listened to the wind harassing the pines overhead and the throb of the creek below. He felt the sturdy little book in his hands and let his thumb ruffle the deckled pages until it found the last poem by feel. He spread the book and opened his eyes. The last poem was called "Winter Brook."

When I climb above the brook flying from purple cliffs,
Through the wind in pines, the lonely bell,
And cross the creek, and climb
into the streaming mists, and past them,
and hear the geese descending in clouds—
When I find myself humming "Sail Returning from Distant Shore"
and feel the cold breath of the snows in the pass,
then I will stop before going over and turn
and I will raise this empty wooden cup to you, my dearest companion:
How many cups of springwater have we shared? How many cups of
    wine?

Tonight I will be so far away. We will not light the candles together.
Tomorrow only the sky and the mountains will be between us.

He read it, and then he repeated it aloud. As if he were talking to his best friend, Wynn, as if Wynn were sitting in the other rocker three feet away. The wooden cup is empty, and he is going over the pass. It was about more than saying one more goodbye, it was about death. Jack knew it. There was no turning around on that mountain trail. And it was about love, and a shared life of friendship, and what that means when facing the end.

He was not surprised that a tear hit the page, nor that he spread it on the paper with his thumb as he had before. Wynn went over without time to say goodbye, to raise any kind of cup, to tell his mother or his little sister, Jess, that he loved them, to thank his father for the times they boiled maple sap all night together in the sugar house. Wynn's eyes looked at Jack with an empty terror as he bled out, then looked past him to the sky. Was it his fault? Jack's? Yes. They had made an unspoken vow to take care of each other first, a vow they renewed with each foray into whitewater or into the mountains, and he had not done it. He had put his distrust of strangers before the life of his friend.

Jack's uncle Lloyd was one of his favorite people. He was his father's older brother, and they split their own parents' ranch down the middle, so Lloyd lived a mile down the valley and the brothers ran their two herds together in the mountains, and helped each other irrigate and hay. Where Pop was reticent and rarely spoke unless circumstances required, Lloyd was the born storyteller whose embellishments were often the point of a tale, and who seemed to live two lives at once: the one on the ground, where cows were fed and fish were caught, and the one a few feet off the turf, where the swirling mists of Lloyd's imagination would add color and cadence and carry it into a retelling that was never without laughter. It awed Jack. But what Jack loved even more was that when it came to hunting and fishing, or the accomplishments of others, the important details remained true. The trout never grew longer, the antlers never got wider. Pop said that Lloyd had once told him that a great storyteller had to know when never to lie. "Hunting and fishing's so much fun," he said, "only a pissant needs to lie about it." Jack could see that in all his father's dealings with Lloyd— sharing the lease, covering for each other in calving time, and with irrigation—Pop trusted his brother more than any other person on earth. Jack knew that Lloyd made life more fun, it was that simple, and without ever compromising the dead seriousness of it. That was a person to ride the river with.

One thing Lloyd repeated was "Leave no man behind."

"Or cow," he would add, if they were riding after the herd and searching for a stray. And he wasn't joking. Uncle Lloyd had gone straight to the recruiter in Kremmling after high school and signed up and spent the better part of eight years as an Army Ranger. He had done a tour in Afghanistan and one somewhere he couldn't talk about. Jack knew that what Lloyd meant was more than a warrior's creed, it was a reminder that we are entrusted with certain souls, and that we are beholden in a broader sense, as people, to take care of others.

Jack had failed Wynn that way, and had not been able to help his mother. Had precipitated her death. Was he broken? Maybe. Den or Jensen clearly thought so. Didn't matter. What mattered was that he was not going to do it again. This river would not take the life of his client, or the lives of children for that matter. Ken had mentioned kids, and Jack had seen one on the road, and now he needed to know.

•

He heard the crunch of pine needles and Alison came around the corner of the cabin and leaned over the porch and knocked three times on the post.

"Come up," he said. "You're not dressed for fishing."

"Nope." She stepped up, put her hands on the hips of her jeans, and surveyed the view—from the wooded wall of the canyon on the other side of the river that was catching the late sun, and down to the dark pool and the flurry of whitewater and the slice of left-turning bend. "Good," she said. "A person could sit here a good long time."

"What I thought when I first arrived." He nodded to the other rocker. She sat and creaked back in the chair and gave it a few test tips. She said, "If I were in a summer dress this would be a country song for sure."

"Kinda."

"Out of sorts?" she said.

"A little."

"Me, too. Why I wasn't up for fishing."

"Want a cup of tea?"

"Sure."

He pushed up out of the chair and laid the book on the tree stump that served as side table. He opened the screen door and eased it closed behind him so it wouldn't clap. From the porch she heard the blurred notes of the kettle filling, the scrape of a steel striker, the double knock of ceramic mugs on wood. If she closed her eyes she could hear the music in almost anything. And everyone moved to a different beat and a different key, and so many used words to try to cover the score, but Jack didn't. She was beginning to get accustomed to Jack's rhythms and she liked them, a lot. She picked up the book beside her and read the cover and opened it to a random page.

THE GUIDE

AFTER LI PO AND LI SHANGYIN

The moon doesn't keep track of how many cups I drink.
She bobs along on the river of stars unconcerned with my sorrow.
I once had a beau whose voice touched me like falling blossoms.
We were just kids and we couldn't wait to make a life together.
We got married and the moon sailed behind us.
What happened? If you came through the gate this evening
I would tell you how the nights have gone silent without your
     laughter.
I will never again hear the sound of your horse clapping up the
     road.
I want so much to tell you how I remember you tonight—
You are my first and only love.

It will have to wait until we meet again on the far side of Star River.
Until then, let's not forget each other.

She shut the book and closed her eyes again. Why did the gentle lines hit her like a blow? The innocence in them, she thought. Distilled and pure. All she was ever trying to do with her music: find something true and distill it, and song had always been the best way. For her. Love was another way, wasn't it? But it never held still long enough. No more than the rush of the river below or the trout that wriggled out of her hands. But for this poet it had, at least on that night of moon and stars and wine.

She could really use a drink. One of Ginnie's mojitos would hit the spot right now. That would have to wait till dinner.

She heard the spring on the screen door yaw and she set the book back on the stump and took the cup of tea Jack handed to her. She could smell it almost like a campfire, Lapsang souchong. He sat and cricked the cane of the chair. She smiled thanks but he didn't see. He was letting his eyes rove over the opposite slope.

"I've been thinking," he said.

"You have?" This time when she said it, it wasn't coy.

"Why would they have a high security fence, arms at the top facing inward, and a big steel gate with code, and dogs downstream and shooters upstream if . . . ?"

"If what?"

"If there's the whole side of the canyon open to the north. And why would they have all that stuff anyway?"

"For celebrities, right? And billionaires. Billionaire's Mile. Isn't that what Shay said? To keep the paparazzi, et cetera, out?"

"Yeah, maybe."

She took a short sip of the tea and set it next to the book. Still too hot. "Good," she said. "With milk and honey, my favorite. Like liquid smoke."

"Me, too."

"But what?" she said.

"Something bad happened to Ken. Cameras everywhere, even over my bed. 'Merc.' What's a merc? Ken said he saw one and they saw him. Mercenaries." Jack blew on the tea. "I bet they're wearing black." He sipped, set the mug in his lap. "And the Takagis are the least addicted-seeming people I've ever seen. He looked guilty asking for a beer at lunch."

•

They sipped their tea in silence. He had brought out a spoon and set it on the stump and she picked it up and fished out the tea bag and wound the string around it to squeeze the hot liquid out of it. The first swallows appeared in the canyon and flashed green as they hit a swath of sunlight.

"So did you come to any conclusions?" she said, finally.

"Yes."

She tipped the chair forward and turned.

"It's not a rehab. That's A."

"What is it?"

"I don't know."

"What's B?"

"They're not worried about fencing the north side of the canyon because over there there's no way out."

"I thought you said it was miles of rough country."

"That's why. There's no help that way. No roads, no traffic, no farms. Not for miles. Just deep drainages and steep ridges.

They've got a pack of dogs and the shepherds are for tracking. They'd be on you in an hour."

She swallowed hard and leaned back, followed his eyes across the canyon.

"So you really think all this is to keep us *in*?"

He didn't say anything.

"Well, then why did they let us go to town? Twice. Go out to fish the other side of the big valley?"

He said, "I think they've made a big investment here. I'm not sure what kind. And I think they'll keep you in when they need to keep you in. Ken—who, it turns out, is not a hen at all—couldn't get out."

"Christ."

"I know."

"Was there a C?"

"I think you should leave. Now. Tomorrow. While you can. Maybe catch the same flight as the Takagis took today."

•

They drank the tea slowly and let the sun go over the ridge downstream and watched the swallows dart in the deepening shade. They walked down to the lodge at 6:20—they weren't in the mood for small talk at the bar—and were surprised to see the Takagis being seated by Shay at a table close to the hearth. If the usually self-possessed young couple had seemed shaken before, now they were determinedly grim. Which was more frightening. They made no effort to meet the eyes of the other guests or force a smile. Sir Will and Neave, and the Fleeces were all standing at the corner of the bar, about to leave it, and taking refills from Ginnie and talking in convivial tones.

Why weren't the Takagis on their flight out of Gunnison? On their way to Denver and another flight to faraway Japan? Alison glanced at them and looked away tactfully and was making her way to her usual table in the far corner by the window when Jack put a hand on her arm.

"Just a sec," he said. "I want to ask them what happened."

"You think that's a good idea?"

"It's my only idea."

She shrugged and they made their way to the hearth and the couple. They were two feet from their table and the startled Takagis when they heard the heavy door open and felt the gust of cool evening air and heard the *clomp* of a boot on boards. Kurt.

His voice when he lifted it had a frayed, resonant edge. "Evening all," he said. The chatter hushed. Everyone turned. Ginnie wiped her hands on a towel and reached to turn down the volume on the iPad under the bar. "Good news and bad news," Kurt said. "Sorry to sound corny." He took off his fawn cowboy hat and held it in front of him as if he were about to deliver a eulogy. "Bad news first, like in every movie, I guess."

Now Teiji touched Jack's elbow and did force a smile and motioned the two of them to sit down in the empty seats. Alison whispered, "Thank you," and Kurt boomed, "Miss K, not a good idea. In fact if you and your guide could step back six feet that would be the best thing. You'll know why in a second."

Alison stiffened. She was confused, and she did not take orders from Kurt Jensen. "Please," he said in his horse trainer's softening register. "It's for the safety of the Takagis."

Alison and Jack stepped back toward the middle of the room. Jensen cleared his throat. "The bad news is that we are on lockdown. This morning they conducted a PanPop test of Crested Butte and found nineteen new cases. Gunnison is seventy-two. Everyone is under Level Three lockdown. Nobody is to leave the lodge property until satellite testing is completed next Monday. I talked to County Health and the vans will arrive Monday just after breakfast. They can have results within the hour. They are stretched very thin, as you can imagine."

A collective murmur rose in the room. Kurt raised his broad hand. "The good news is that the kitchen is well stocked and the fishing is as good as I've ever seen it." Jack couldn't help a wince. Who else here was fishing? "And everyone here is scheduled to fly out Monday anyway," Kurt continued. "So as long as the test results come in clear, which I have no doubt they will, there will be no more interruptions to anyone's schedule." Jack saw Sir Will raise a glass of amber on ice, probably bourbon, and mutter, "Here, here."

Kurt turned bodily toward the center of the dining area where Alison and Jack stood. "It's come to my attention that Miss K and her guide visited a crowded bar in Crested Butte yesterday evening, so I am going to have to ask you both to be respectful of social distancing. When I talked to County and advised them of our numbers and ventilation system, they said that so long as you eat at your usual table fifteen feet from the rest, and maintain that distance from the others as best you can, we should be fine. I thank you now for your cooperation, as do the rest of the guests, I'm sure."

That was it. Another coup counted. Jensen was isolating the two of them. Any plans of early departure were quashed, and any gleaning of intel from the others was now essentially impossible. *Well played, you asshole,* Jack thought.

•

After dinner they left quickly and he walked her to her cabin. Once on the sandy road, under a half moon in clouds, and accompanied by the spinning and ticking of the aspen leaves on the slope, he said,

"I'm not just gonna sit here and wait for something really bad to happen."

She squeezed his arm. "What are you gonna do?"

"He's outmaneuvering us. He's pushing us into a corner of the corral, and toward a squeeze chute. I can feel it. He took my rifle, he took my phone—"

"What?" she said.

"I discovered it after lunch today. I left it in the chest pocket of my waders like I always do, and when I took them off the peg after lunch it was gone. Yeah, I know: not so bright."

"Crap." Now she took his hand and they continued up the road slowly.

He said, "Rifle, phone, and now they have a reason to lock us in. Brilliant. And not to talk to the others. Who knows if any of it is even true. We're getting separated, cut out of the herd, like I said. Like two steers bound for the packing plant."

He felt her hand tighten on his. In the shade of a big ponderosa he stopped. "My uncle Lloyd was an Army Ranger. He's a lot louder than Pop and way better in a bar fight. He always told me that when you are getting edged into a bad beating, when there's only one outcome—which you know is you on the floor bleeding with something broke—keep acting like you're getting edged, then strike first and fast."

"Seems like common sense."

He smiled. "It is. But hardly anybody does it. I guess people are too hopeful."

"Hunh." She searched his eyes. "But we don't know anything. At all. Not really."

"I know, that's what I mean. Hopeful. We know enough."

She was trying not to be scared now, trying not to buy in—to the conviction that they were really in danger. But she was also outraged. Good. "So?" she said.

"So I've gotta go in."

"In?"

"To Kreutzer's. To see what the fuck is going on. Really."

"Isn't that what Ken did?"

"Yes."

She grimaced. "Then what?"

"I don't know." He walked her to her cabin, up to the porch, and at her door he leaned in. Her hair was soft on her neck and she smelled like trees and wind. He kissed her neck. "See you at breakfast," he said.

•

When he got back to his cabin he glanced at the Nest thermostat and thought there was no way he would sleep knowing Den or Jensen could be watching him stretched on the bed. So he got his fishing pack from the porch, and set it on the quilt, and under the light of the sconces he took out three fly boxes, two large and one small, and acted like he was making a selection for the next morning. Then he packed the boxes away and set the pack on the bureau smack in front of the thermostat. "There, you peeping motherfuckers," he mouthed to himself. Then he set the alarm on his watch and set it to vibrate and stuck the watch under his ear and slept like a rock.

•

The hum in his ear woke him at 5:00. He dressed fast in his usual fishing outfit, splashed water on his face, took his cap off the nail, and stepped into the predawn dark. Cold. He zipped up the black fleece. The moon had set and there were slow currents of stars. He could smell the pines and the icy breath of the river. He walked up to the teal bike on its kickstand and bounced down to the lodge. Once there he did not dismount and lean the bike on its kickstand and go inside for coffee. Five fifteen by the glow on his watch dial—coffee would not be ready for almost an hour. Shay would not pack her breakfast cart for thirty minutes or so.

He rode right past the porch and with barely enough starlight to see, he found the cart path that ran back up through the aspens on the other side of the pond. He rolled onto it and ped-aled hard. He passed behind the main house—only the security lights burning—and biked across the packed gravel of the parking area—not a soul around, and if anyone stopped him and asked he'd say he had to get some gear out of his truck—and he headed straight toward the big equipment shed. He doglegged around it in the pines, and around the back he could just make out the cart path continuing. So the track went right through the big shed. To any onlooker, it would seem that any-one driving a golf cart into it was stopping there, presumably to offload or pick up some tools or supplies or provisions. But he could see in the very first traces of gray light a garage door on the back side and the track continuing on east, upcanyon, to Kreutzer's. The only place it could be going.

The track stayed in the wide hedgerow of trees that hid the tall fence, parallel to the road. That was good for him because it kept him hidden. When it hit the driveway that cut across the big field, Jack turned up it. He could see a security light on Kreutzer's house, up in the apex of the eaves, maybe three hundred yards away. He biked up the driveway, which was paved with tarmac. Also good, it did not crunch or pop. And when he was about fifty yards from the house he ditched the bike in the tall hay grass and jogged.

At the end of the drive there was a wide circular turnaround bordered with juniper hedge and an Italianate fountain in the middle. That was odd. It was a life-size nymph in gray stone pouring water from a two-handled jar. Also good, because the splashing water covered any sounds his footsteps might have made. The circle was all custom-cut flagstone—that was over-the-top, one had to have money to burn to install a stone turnaround—and there were five vehicles parked there: the windowless white plumbing van he'd seen from the ridge, a black Jeep Cherokee, which he recognized, a shiny black Suburban, and Jensen's black pickup. Also a red Tesla coupe with a Colorado vanity plate sporting the letters RNA.

•

He didn't know what to do. The blinds were drawn in the windows facing the drive. He wanted to circle around back—he remembered that he could see uncovered lights in the big river-facing windows that first night he went scouting. But they

were surveilling that side for sure, that's where stray fisherfolk walked up the bank and across the line and got shot at . . .
He was thinking that when he heard the thud of a metal door.
Unmistakable. And then low voices, rough, and a short excla-
mation of pain and a whimper. And then the scuff and patter of
footsteps. He raised his head just enough to see over the hedge.

The security light lit the turnaround but it was not strong.
And he looked to his right, upcanyon, toward the commotion,
and saw a wide flagstone path leading into thick trees, mostly
black timber. If there was a building in there it was hidden by
the pines; he hadn't seen it from his perch on the ridge. He
strained to see in the grudging twilight and in the gap appeared
two men in black. Black tactical uniforms, black caps, one he
could tell had a light beard and was about the same height and
breadth as the man eating ice cream who had also been driving
the Jeep. And both men carried black M4 assault rifles on
slings. And behind them came an apparition, not seemingly of
this world: a line of pale figures, smaller than the men, moving
unsteadily and wavering as if pushed by wind.

It was a line of people in . . . what? Hospital gowns. Like the girl
yesterday. Off-white or maybe pale blue and festively patterned
with what could have been dogs or lions. Single file, shuffling
their bare legs, their feet, he saw, in cheap hospital slippers.

He might have raised his face too high, he needed to see better,
to understand what he was seeing. As they came out into the
turnaround and passed to his side of the cars he saw that most
were barely adults. Not even. Twelve total, he counted twelve.
Three seemed to be from the same family, two girls and a boy.
They held each other's hands. One girl, very slight, looked to

be about fifteen, if that. She kept turning her head, scanning wildly like a panicked animal being herded onto the slaughter truck, and she was murmuring something in what? Jack thought he recognized Vietnamese. She was the one on the road. Jack would swear it. Did their eyes lock? He thought she might have seen him. The other girl was early twenties maybe, as was the boy. Next a young woman, tawny-skinned, and a boy, younger, who had the same nose and eyes, who might have been her brother. She was holding his hand and half dragging him, and Jack noticed that his skin was gray, his bones prominent, and as he watched, the boy's eyes widened to saucers and he grabbed his side and his face collapsed in pain. *¡Ven, ven, hermanito!* he heard the girl say, desperate, and she tugged, but the boy stopped and collapsed. He curled to the flagstones. It halted the line, and one of the guards in front, compact and dark-haired, broke ranks, strode back, yanked the boy up by his arm, and urged, "You again. C'mon. In a week you can collapse all you want—" And he picked the writhing boy up like a sack of grain and threw him over his shoulder and strode back to the front. Jack noticed that the boy was too weak to even kick and that his sister had begun to sob, silently. A very thin, gangly young man was behind her; he had high cheeks and wide-set bluish eyes which he kept on the ground. A girl after that, late teens, very blond, followed by a tall boy with skin the color of rosewood and maybe his sister, also tall, walking erect despite the wasted cheeks and shiny eyes of what seemed malnutrition. Then a muscular kid covered in tattoos, followed by a tall girl and a short boy, maybe just out of their teens. The girl was emaciated and had a red bindi tattoo on her forehead and a dark birthmark running down the back of her left leg and she was crying. And behind them two more broad-shouldered security dudes in black carrying the automatic carbines. The hospital gowns were tied at the neck and open at the back, and the patients or prisoners were naked underneath, and the thin cotton did not cover their butts as they walked. One of the following guards prodded the weeping girl in her bare back with the barrel of his rifle and Jack heard him say, "Hush now. Time for a big breakfast." He continued to heckle her loudly across the circle. At the double front door with a jumping trout carved in the lintel—Jack recognized it as the same trout by the same artist as the one on the lodge's steel gate—the bearded guard in the lead turned and, irritated, said, "Taggart, keep it down. Guests still sleeping." He pressed his thumb on a keypad and leaned into the heavy alder door and the awful parade filed in. The door swung closed with a decisive and steely click.

Jack retreated through the tall grass. Fuckfuckfuck. The little boy who spoke Spanish, wherever he was from, he was dying. Jack knew it. The rest were, too. More slowly. The weeping girl.

He had to back off. When he got to the bike he righted it and wheeled it around and swung on and sprinted back up the drive. His watch said 5:55. He didn't want to meet Shay on the cart coming up the path but he did. The golf cart had a single headlight and he saw it jouncing toward him through the woods along the fence, and he had plenty of time to swerve into the trees and throw down the bike and crouch until she passed.

•

He collected himself and walked the bike back around the pond as if he had just taken a scenic detour on his way from his cabin. Maybe he was looking for feeding trout on the far bank; no one would question him.

But it was hard to act normally. He stopped well back from the porch and held on to the handlebars. He kept sucking in deep breaths and feeling a spasm in the muscles across his rib cage. When he closed his eyes he saw the ragged line of ghosts in their paltry gowns shuffling out of the darkness of trees into the twilight of a security lamp, uncertain steps, pushed like a sweeping of leaves wind-hurried through an open door. Except it was not wind that hurried them, it was armed men, brawny men who looked and acted like soldiers. Who knew how to control prisoners.

Prisoners. The crying of the tall girl, the hard jab of the gun, the terror on the face of the youngest, readable even in the half-light.

What the hell. In the words of Ken, whom Jack no longer thought of as a Hen. All the things that had not seemed right in the past days led to that spectral parade. Of kids. Because that's what they were. The oldest was probably twenty.

The stillest morning and clear. Even the aspens were silent. It would warm fast and the fish would start feeding early. He sucked in a deep breath. *That's it, think like a guide. Nothing to do right now but fish.* Then he put the bike on its kickstand and went through the door.

•

Alison was at the fire with her coffee. Will and Neave were at their table already, as were the Fleeces, and the Takagis were nowhere to be seen. Maybe taking breakfast in their cabin. Jack wondered again what they had seen that had so derailed them, and thought that it must have something to do with children and young adults in hospital gowns.

He and Alison walked wide around the two other tables, respecting the new mandate to distance, and the couples smiled stiffly, which accentuated the sense of being pariahs. Jensen knew what he was about and Jack hated him then. Before, the man's gruffness and plays at dominance had aggravated him, but he'd been around many men like Kurt and in the world he navigated he expected them. But now he felt the deliberate moves of a wolf, angling to cull his prey from the herd; and now that he had seen that line of kids, Jack couldn't tolerate it. He wouldn't.

They sat at their usual table in the corner and barely spoke. Shay slipped a cloth mask from her throat over her nose when she approached their table and she made no conversation as she served almond croissants and coffee and asked how they would like their eggs cooked.

When Shay was gone, Jack said, "I took a bike ride this morning. Tell you about it on the river." Alison was breaking the croissant and did not look up but he could see that she'd heard him. When he saw Shay coming back with the coffeepot he said to Alison, "It will warm fast today. The first hour may have the best fishing. Let's eat and go."

"Fine by me. Better than fine."

Bacon and eggs. All-American breakfast. They did not ask for another refill on coffee, nor did Jack ask Shay for the usual morning fishing snacks. They laid their cloth napkins on the table, pushed back, and left the lodge without looking back.

•

Who knew if the Takagis would fish. Or continue their "treatments." Jack and Alison would start all the way downstream and fish up. He wanted to take another look at Ellery's fence anyway. Alison seemed game to try anything, if not excited as on her first mornings. Well, this is what fishing was for, wasn't it?

All his life, when things had gotten really tough, or confusing, or almost too beautiful to bear, Jack had gone fishing. He had fished through every joy and heartbreak. Fished when his mother died, when Cheryl had told him she loved him more than anything, when he had gotten into Dartmouth. He had fished after he lost Wynn, and fished when his father told him gently to come home. He had learned that it was much less a distraction than a form of connection: of connecting to the best part of himself, and to a discipline that demanded he stay open to every sense, to the nuances of the season and to the instrument of his own body, his own agility or fatigue. Above all it asked him to commit the whole of his attention, which he decided is the only way he truly knew how to love anything.

So whatever the hell was going on at the lodge, whatever perverse moves Jensen—or the elusive Den—had up his sleeve, there was not a damn thing to do this morning except fish. Often, when Jack bumped up against an intractable problem, he found that after a long session on the stream he had a solution.

They picked up their rods and jogged down the steps, and when they hit the river trail they turned downstream.

•

The prettiest trail. On any other late summer morning the slide of the bends, the gravel bars where white moths flitted in and out of sunlight and landed on purple asters—it would have made a heart sing. But this morning they walked as if they were going to a job neither particularly wanted to do. Halfway to the fence line, Jack turned through an opening in the alders and waded into the current. A few feet off the bank it poured over a wide boulder and threshed white with a loud rush. No one would hear them out there. She followed and they stood knee deep and shoulder to shoulder in a pool infused with bubbles from the pourover. He pulled his waist pack around to the front, opened it, and talked as he selected a fly.

"Like I said, this morning I took a bike ride."

"Okay."

"I'm gonna tell you something rough. But look like I'm explaining all about nymphing. Okay?"

"Okay."

He told her. About taking his bike up the canyon in the dark and about what he saw from the grass.

He said, "They were in hospital gowns, naked underneath. They were terrified. One got prodded in the back. One I'm sure was the girl from the road. I've helped load pigs into the slaughter truck and that's what they looked like." He had trouble going on. Alison caught herself staring at him, waiting for him to continue, and remembered to unhook yesterday's dry fly from the keeper and cut it free with her nippers. As she did she said, "You recognized two of the guards from Crested Butte?"

"Yes. At least one."

"How old were the patients?"

"Patients? I'm not sure that's what I'd call them. Maybe fifteen to twenty. Twenty-one. All young."

"All you think from someplace else? Like newly arrived?"

"They had that look. When the boy fell and the girl got hit, two of them exclaimed in Spanish. The youngest was saying something to herself in what I think was Vietnamese, I'm not sure."

Alison didn't say anything. She couldn't look at him or the fly he was tying on. She couldn't look anywhere but at the river. Out here in the bright sun, the stream was all glistening rocks, spilling burble. He saw her chest rising and falling. "You think it's sex trafficking? For addicted billionaires?"

"I don't know. It didn't seem like that kind of group. I mean they were in hospital gowns and like cardboard slippers and they seemed . . . I don't know . . . weak. You remember the girl on the road."

She watched the river. If she was seeing anything at all. He'd never seen her so contained. She seemed to be listening to the strains of the current as if to a distant flute.

"And like I said, I'm not sure addiction has anything to do with it. Despite Shay's nondisclosure thing."

Finally Alison said, "Are we gonna go get in your truck and screw Jensen's lockdown and drive to the sheriff?"

Jack finished tying on the second nymph, bit off the tail end of tippet, and took off his cap. He rubbed his forehead with the sleeve of his shirt. "That's just it. I told you I saw a squad car running sweep into the gate the other day. And the one out on the road apprehending the girl. That's just what we can't do."

"Huh?" She turned. "Is that what you think? The locals are in on it? All the law?"

Jack shrugged. "I don't know what *it* is. All I know is these guys aren't fucking around. Jensen and Cody both made a point of saying that the sheriff wouldn't touch the crazy shit going on around here. And then I see that car. One misstep and I'm guessing we're toast." He snugged his cap back on. "Also, it's hearsay or whatever. If I'd had my phone, I was so shocked I probably would've forgotten to take a pic anyway. These are serious dudes, with serious money. Even if you went to the law you'd have to have pics, something. And Ken . . . there's nothing. All I saw was an old boot."

Her eyes flashed. He saw the heat in her face. It wasn't a girlish blush. "I've got a guy," she said.

"You do?"

"Yep. His name is Vincent Serra. You met him."

"I did?"

"Remember? The head of my security when I'm on tour? That first night?"

"Oh, yeah."

"He's my friend."

Jack said, "Cast while you tell me. I never know when we're on frigging camera. Let's work downstream, so cast across and let them swing down."

•

She fished and as the flies drifted, and as she lifted her rod and tightened the line for a roll cast, she said, "He was FBI. Division chief at the San Francisco field office. He knows everyone everywhere. We never have a single problem on tour. Not with local police or gangs or bikers or anyone."

"Whoa."

"Yep. He came to one of my concerts twelve years ago, when I was just breaking out. It was in a band shell down in the Presidio. He came backstage afterward and flashed that gold badge. 'Am I under arrest?' I said. He said, 'Only if you ever stop singing.' He said it was the best version of 'Boulder to Birmingham' he'd ever heard. He said he cried. And then he said, 'I'm retiring in two years, and I'm gonna be the head of your security. If you let me. I'm house-trained and I don't eat too much.' " She laughed. It surprised Jack—the gust of mirth. "Well, that was sort of a lie. He can eat an eighteen-inch pizza for a snack." She cast again.

"Ha. I could eat a pizza about now. Comfort food."

"If we got him pics he could call it in. He'd do anything for me, but he has a way of getting his ducks in a row first."

Jack whistled. He thought, "Not *we*. *We* don't get pics, I do." He thought how he'd probably already endangered her by over-sharing. How he was getting her in deeper and deeper. Wasn't that what he always did? Run his people into danger. He said, "I'll get pics. Tomorrow morning. Would the line of kids be enough?"

"I don't know."

"Me neither." I know less and less about anything, he thought. And then he said, "Doesn't matter, you need to leave. Like today."

She reeled in, swung the bottom fly into her left hand, and stepped back so she was facing him. "I told you, I can't go home. And you know what?" He shook his head. "Nothing on earth I can't stand worse than a bully. Or a user."

Jack didn't say anything. She wasn't done. "When I was coming up, I saw shit that would make you ballistic. Young women of real, raw talent twisted and bulldogged into people—things— they were not. Women silenced and used. They tried it on me and guess what?"

He felt the icy current pressing his knees.

"They screwed with the wrong outfit. I don't walk away from it now or turn my back. On anything like it."

Well, Jack thought, they had that in common. He had been suspended from high school for knocking flat the star quarterback, who had just stomped and spit on a new boy from Chihuahua, Mexico.

Jack blinked against the sun. "Okay," he whispered. Then he said out loud, "I guess. Let's reel in and head down to the fence. I want to take another look anyway."

"I don't really feel like fishing much, but okay."

She held her rod up and turned and they waded out of the sun and into the shade of the bank.

•

They found the path again. The trail wound through the leaning spruce and emerged in a grove of poplars whose leaves spun in sunlight like chimes, and it ended abruptly in a barbed-wire fence. The four strands of barbed wire were stretched tight right across the creek on stout posts. Which Jack was certain was illegal—blocking a navigable waterway, navigable by kayak certainly—but ranchers did it all the time. Nothing else unusual. Except the knowledge of dogs, which were wholly vicious by the sound of it. Or was that part even true?

"Guess we'll start again here," he said.

She'd been carrying her own rod despite his insistence that it was part of a guide's job, but she let him take it and unhook the bead-head pheasant tail from the keeper and yank six feet of line off the reel in two quick tugs and break the fly off in his teeth. He did the same with the fly higher up, and then he reached for a wooly bugger streamer that was hooked to a patch of foam on the outside of his waist pack. He held the two inches of streamlined black fur in the sunlight so that she could see the threads of sparkle and the weighted brass eyes that had been tied into the soft minnow mimic. "Wanna try a streamer this morning? A whole new tactic. You'll strip it in like a wounded minnow."

"I feel a little like a wounded minnow. Fuck Jensen."

"Okay, then you won't even be pretending."

She twisted her lips and was very glad to be with someone who could find a shred of humor on a morning like this. If Jack's father had his maxims, so did Alison's mother. Her mother had been a nurse in Murphy when one stripped slope of the copper mine outside of Ducktown collapsed and killed seventeen men and injured dozens more. Mama K always said, "Laughter makes you tougher." Short and sweet, which is just how the woman was herself.

She was thinking that when she heard the barking. Not barking so much as pitched yelps and yowls. Not just one dog, but maybe half a dozen, more. Sounded like a frenzied coyote pack cornering a hurt elk. Jack dropped the hand that held the fly and their heads came up. It came from beyond the fence, from Ellery's somewhere.

"Good God," Alison said.

"What I was thinking."

"Sounds like frigging murder."

"Hold on." Jack handed her the rod and dropped the fishing pack.

"What are you doing?" she said.

"Sick of wondering about everything. I'll just be a minute."

Her jaw dropped. "You're going in there? What about the mastiffs?"

"Exactly. Don't worry, after this morning I'm not going anywhere without this." He unzipped his waist pack and showed her the black Glock 26 nestled between two fly boxes. "Jensen doesn't know about this one. I've carried it in my truck since I was sixteen."

She nodded. He unbuckled the waist pack and shoved the handgun under his safety belt at the back of his waders and pulled the camo tech shirt down over it. "Be right back. Please don't move." He stepped to the fence, stopped, turned back. "Almost forgot. Lemme borrow your phone."

She dug it out swiftly from a large side pocket of her vest.

"It swipes to camera, right?"

She nodded.

" 'Kay, be right back."

He grabbed the top of the nearest post and used the third strand of wire like the rung of a ladder and, careful not to tear his waders on the barbs, he vaulted the four-foot fence like he'd done it a million times, which he had. And was gone.

He ran. Open woods here, fern under the aspen, and he turned away from the creek and ran up the hill toward the clamor. Within a hundred yards it benched out and he was weaving fast through pinewoods and then he saw the barn at the edge of the field and smelled the familiar scents of horses, manure, saw-dust. He could see through the straight trunks of the lodgepole the packed dirt yard and off to the right the circular rail fencing of a corral and to the right of that, and connected by a chute, the high shiplap walls of maybe a squeeze chute for vet work, but it wasn't. It had four walls about seven feet high and no roof, it was some kind of pen . . . and he caught the movement from the barn.

He bent low and ran forward tree to tree to get a better look and froze. Two men in black caps, not the bearded one, were dragging someone out of the barn by the armpits. Whoever it was had long black hair that dragged in the dirt and her head lolled—he could see now it was a she—and she was naked and unresponsive. She was emaciated, too, Jack could see her ribs like stripes in the bright sunlight and then he saw the purple birthmark running down the back of her leg. It was the girl from the morning, the one with the bindi, the one who had been weeping. And Jack knew she was dead. Something in the way her legs bounced over the ruts, in the loll of her head and the color of her arms. And somehow, with the dogs whining and yelping, and the image of death running before him, he thought to pull Alison's cell phone from the chest pocket of his waders, which he'd folded down. He unzipped and pulled it out and began snapping pictures. The men were in no hurry. They dragged the body of the girl across the yard and disappeared behind the board wall and then Jack heard a shout and a change in pitch from whines to snarls and tortured barks and a ripping that he could never unhear.

•

He made himself back up. Made himself work across the level bench tree to tree, made himself move one foot, then another. But he stumbled once in the clumsy waders over a blowdown branch, and he made himself stop, one hand on a tree, and breathe.

Once he was over the hill, he ran and skidded down through the trees to the river and entered the aspen grove and clambered over the fence. She stood from her seat on a sandstone block.

"What's wrong?" she said.

"I . . . We thought . . ." Fuck it. He unzipped the wader pocket, tapped the phone, handed it to her.

"What is it?" She turned herself so the phone was in the shade. "A barn?" She spread two fingers over the photo. "It's . . . Oh." She froze. "A girl?" He nodded. "The dogs? The frenzy of the dogs?" He nodded. "One of the girls from . . . ?"

"Yes."

"Was she—?"

"I think she was dead. I hope so."

"Oh." Alison sat back on the rock, gagged. A dry heave and she pressed her forearm over her eyes for a second. When she looked at him it was as if every passion in her had distilled and her eyes held a clarified anger he could barely meet. She said, "The girl is wasted. Away, I mean. She looks starved."

"The others didn't look much better."

"I—" She sat. Jack heard the morning wind spin the leaves in the canopy. He saw the track of a tear on her cheek. "A young girl. What the hell is going on up there?" she said.

"What the hell is going on down *here*? This is supposed to be 'Ellery's.' None of it is true. It's all part of the lodge and it's all a lie."

"Part of what?" she said. "Doesn't matter. We have a photo. We can go straight to town and text it—"

She stopped herself. Probably thinking about the deputy and the girl on the road, and the squad car going through the gate at Kreutzer's—how that was one thing they definitely could not do.

"Look," he said. "We'll find a way." Did he believe it? His heart was hammering. He scanned the woods, the riverbank. Once he and Pop had hunted the Gore Range in November. He'd walked out along a drifted ridge in a light blowing snow and when he walked back in the evening he saw that his tracks had been covered most of the way by a big mountain lion. He felt that way now.

"I think we should fish. In case somebody's watching," he said. "Try to act normal. We gotta get through this morning. We'll fish."

"Okay," she said. "Then what?"

"We fish up to the lodge before lunch. Then we walk to my truck to get some gear. Streamer boxes. You say out loud you're curious to see the dam and tailwater upstream, no harm in that, lockdown or no. 'Cause you're always a rebel. Then we make a break for it."

She was looking at him like a little kid who wants to believe a fairy tale. He picked up the rod again and found the end of the tippet he'd dropped fifteen minutes before and tried to focus on tying on the fly. It was not a small hook but it took him several attempts to thread the eye.

CHAPTER TWELVE

Jack was never good at hiding his emotions. Or faking them. He was never, for instance, in a high school play. What you saw was what you got. Now he wanted out and he wanted to bring her with him, and he wanted to bust whatever was happening here as fast as he could. With a call or text to the right person or not. Barring that, he wanted to kill. The men in black and Jensen to start with. Den foremost. Once he and Uncle Lloyd had driven up to Craig to watch Jack's cousin Zane ride bareback broncs at the July Fourth rodeo. They were walking the dusty fairgrounds during the kids' mutton busting and they came around the corner of a four-horse trailer and saw a team roper yanking the head of his gelding around by the bit. Hard. Too hard. The horse's mouth was frothing and his eyes were wild and the man was hissing and growling. Lloyd stepped up and tapped the man's shoulder and when he turned he decked him. A mouth punch that must've broken the man's jaw. "How's that feel?" he said to the roper, who was coming to all fours and dripping blood into the dirt. Lloyd turned and took the reins and stroked the dun's neck and walked him straight to the event vet and said, "I'd like to report horse abuse." He didn't need a photo, the horse's mouth was bleeding.

As they walked away from the doc's trailer, Lloyd turned to Jack and said, "Some people need killing. Simple as that." Jack never forgot it.

They fished upstream, riffle to riffle, pool to pool, and for the first time in his life Jack could not connect—either to the water or to Alison's movements—he followed in a trance, and she forced the heavy streamer and casted too fast and tangled her line every third throw. But they kept at it, and they stopped thigh-deep in a long eddy and ate a trail bar Jack had in his pack and shared a quart of Gatorade. And fished on. At 11:15 they walked up the steps and hung their waders at the corner of the porch and put their rods in the rack to be ready for an afternoon fish, and Jack said loudly, "Let's get a good variety of streamers. I've got two boxes in my truck. It'll be a good education." And she nodded and they walked up the sandy, needle-strewn road to the parking area by the gate. As they walked, he looked up into the aspen on the slope and saw, on the porch of one of the empty cabins, a figure standing stock-still. It was Cody, and he was watching their progress with zero expression.

They got to the back of his truck and he found the key to the topper in his pocket and swung up the windowed hatch and called, "We'll get streamers and we'll try some crawdads, too. Why not."

And she stood back and looked at the sport watch on her wrist and said, "Hey, we've got over half an hour till lunch. Let's go up and look at the dam. No harm in that. I've heard the tailwater is a legendary fishery."

"Sure," he called. "Why not?" He glanced at his watch. "We've got time. Better get a move on. Here. The numbers to the keypad." He lifted his chin to the gate and tossed her the tag Kurt had given him the first afternoon. "I'll close up and pick you up."

He took the fly boxes from the back. Also from the plastic bucket his fencing tool—which was a hammer, staple puller, heavy-duty pliers, and wire cutter all in one—and two sticks of dynamite, which he stuck in his waistband under his shirt. He locked the handle to the topper, climbed into the driver's seat. Started the truck. Pressed the electric opener and slid down his window. Put the truck in reverse. And looked up in time to see her punch the numbers on the keypad on its post, then punch them again. Then turn to face him, her hand to her mouth in naked fear. The gate had not budged.

•

Jack picked up the fly boxes, locked his door, held the new gear where it was visible, and without a word they walked back down the track to lunch. Up ahead a path fed into the sand road from the cabins on the slope, and the Takagis were coming down it, hand in hand, almost in a trance. The wind was moving in the trees, bending the limbs and rushing the leaves, but they didn't seem to notice. They moved as if they were heading to a proceeding they did not much care for. And when they joined the track and noticed Jack and Alison, they startled and forced a smile and there was an awkward moment when all four put on face masks and the Takagis gestured for them to go first, but Alison insisted. And so the four of them walked down to the lodge, two by two, with the Takagis leading by a few feet.

Jack now felt cornered and more than ever he knew he had nothing to lose. He said loud enough for the Takagis to hear, "We saw the kids. In their hospital gowns."

Did the Takagis hitch and stop for just a second? Yes. Then they walked.

"One girl was just murdered and fed to dogs."

Another hitch, a slight turn of the ear. He could only see the backs of their heads.

"We saw it," Jack continued. "What the hell is going on here. Time to say. *Now*. And keep walking like nobody's talking."

"I—We can't . . . We . . ." Yumi stammered.

"It's time," Jack said. The harsh authority in his own words surprised him. "Children are being murdered."

They were all walking slowly. Yumi cleared her throat. Hesitated. "We were told," Yumi said, just loud enough. Lucky she was wearing a mask—a camera would not know they were conversing. She spoke in a rush. "We were told they were volunteers, that they and their families were being compensated beyond their wildest dreams. We . . . asked about the restraints when they hooked them up to the machines, the bruising. All those machines . . ."

Now Teiji. "We were told that the transfusions can cause convulsions, harmless in themselves. But that the restraints prevented self-harm. It is clear this is not the case."

"What the hell is going on?" Jack said again.

"Plasma," Teiji said.

"Plasma," Jack muttered, but they heard him.

"Super immunity," Teiji said. "From all disease. Live survivor plasma. In very few . . . special subjects." He was having uncharacteristic trouble organizing his thoughts. "Also the possibility of reverse aging. As shown in rats."

"As shown in rats," Jack repeated. It was all he could muster. And to keep a straight line. His mind was reeling. He was thinking about the girl, how thin she was. The small boy convulsing. For how many rounds did they use them before they were wrung out? But now the group was only twenty-five yards from the front porch and the lodge and so Jack raised his voice and said, "Streamers *are* tough, but we think we'll have good luck down below again this afternoon."

•

He had said it without thinking, but realized during lunch he had set a plan in motion. They would "fish" below, again. The dogs were kenneled up in the shed off the barnyard. The disposal shed. He and Alison would go straight over the fence, straight downriver to the next property or the next, and steal a car and run. They'd text pics to Vince on the way. Extreme urgency. The little boy didn't have long, Jack was sure of it.

On the deck it was windier than any lunch had been. The breeze came flat downstream and swayed the tops of the pines, presaging maybe another storm, so they picked a new table against the lodge wall. Also, Jack thought their regular tables might be bugged. Was he paranoid? Definitely not. *Super immunity. Reverse aging.* He kept hearing the words. Alison's fury vibrated like a pot at full boil. Under her breath, between spoonfuls of cold consommé, she said, "Special subjects, Jesus. I read about it. The plasma of Covid survivors led to the study of those who had survived things like West Nile and dengue. They're getting them from all over the world, Jack. They must be paying off nurses and docs from Saigon to Mexico City."

Jack spread his hand above the tablecloth with a motion downward: Let's not talk about it now. Let's focus on leaving. He couldn't stop thinking about the term *live survivor plasma*. The images of Band-Aids on the backs of hands, of tubes running between billionaires and broken children. For some reason he kept thinking about Wynn's sugar lot, the maple sap–gathering operation Wynn's dad ran in Vermont in March and April, the crisscrossing clear plastic tubes running from tree to tree and down the slopes to the gathering tanks. Den wasn't selling syrup, he was selling immortality. Or the closest thing money could buy. Jack tried not to look—at the knighted windmill mogul leaning affably toward his . . . whatever she was, maybe talking about what they would do with years and years of beaming health; the blond couple chattering away in a patch of sunlight.

But he did look, and before his eyes they morphed into vampires.

He and Alison finished the meal, took the waders from the pegs, and geared up; took down the rods; Jack checked his waist pack as if for flies and confirmed he had the Glock. Then they went down the steps with the speed of eager fisherpeople.

Down the trail without stopping. Through the grove of poplars to the barbed-wire fence. Over the river the steel strands
gleamed in sunlight. It occurred to him then that barbed wire
would not stop vicious dogs, that the mastiffs would jump it as
the deer did, or crawl under or through like bears. Why didn't
they? Because there must be an invisible fence as well, the dogs
must wear shock collars. But they were in the shed, so.

"Hold on." Jack thought about his thermostat.

No way they wouldn't have a camera down here. They were
still twenty feet from the fence and he scanned the trees, the
limbs around them. He squatted low in the middle of the trail,
leaned far forward so he could see three more trunks and he
saw it. The camo-printed strapping. It was at knee height,
around a poplar set back from the trail, but with an opening
forward toward the fence. The wind was thrashing in the canopy, coming downstream, which was not usual in the afternoons. It meant a weather front. Good. Because the brush was
moving, too. Jack approached the tree and from behind and
above he could see the plastic rectangle of the game camera.
Also printed in camo. The perfect, least obvious device, set to
record only when there was movement in front of it. They used
them on the ranch often, to see when the coyotes or bears came
down to harass the new calves. Jack would not shoot them as
his neighbors did, but if they were around in calving season
he would often take his tent and sleep in the pasture with the
dogs. The camera here would not just produce a video to be
retrieved later, it would be wired in to Wi-Fi or a transmitter for a
live feed.

He reached up and broke a dense dry limb off a spruce that was among the poplars and when a gust flattened the leaves of the trees on the other side of the fence he threw the limb down sideways across the camera as if blown. Good. A mass of lacy twigs covered the lens.

"Okay," he said to her. "We're good."

He'd put the fencing tool and dynamite in his waist pack and now he fished out the heavy red-handled cutters and snipped the strands between two posts. No sound of dogs, good. She watched him. "You think they have another camera?" she said, scanning the trees.

"Maybe," he said. "We're gonna have to move fast."

"Should we bring the rods?" she said. "The waders?"

He hesitated. "Yes. It's always an alibi. We couldn't resist . . ."

"Okay."

He motioned her into the gap. She made herself smile and walked through.

"Hold on," he said. The lowest strand lay unsprung and curled around her foot. She held on. She scanned the shadowed woods ahead for movement. Animal movement. He bent to untangle the wire and pull it back and never got up.

CHAPTER THIRTEEN

The smack flashed a jag of light, then darkness. Thud of pain, back of head. Taste of mineral grit and moss.

He knew he had been toppled by a blow. The corner of his mouth, right side, was in the trail. Through the throb of blood in his ears he could hear a startled cry and slap. He tried to open an eye, the one not in dirt. He did. Blurry. He saw a tall figure, just a shape, yanking Alison around by her hair, saw another arm go back against the sky and strike her. Then the voice.

"I always liked your music, I did. Kinda slutty, though, I always thought. Nothin' but love songs, I figure she's gotta be a slut, and damn if I weren't dead-on. God." Hearing still good, Jack heard a loud spit. Cody. What the fu—And he saw the free hand go to her face, heard her gurgled groan, because now he had her by the throat.

The shot popped. Not the narrow crack of a rifle but a round report, almost like a rock hitting rock. And Jack saw the tall shadow stagger back and double over and then he, Cody, hit the dirt. He was humped less than ten feet away.

And then she was on him, on Jack, lifting his head in both hands, saying, "Jesus, Jesus, you okay? You okay? God*damn*. Please please don't be mortally wounded, I swear I'll be mad."

And Jack moaned out as best he could, but the words garbled, and she was peeling off her torn shirt and holding it to the back of his head, pressing it with one hand while the other reached for a strap on the pack and hauled it to her and worked out the water bottle and then she was pouring cold water on the back of his head where her hand had been and she was saying, "That lowlife bastard, that fucker, I knew, I *knew* he was bad medicine. *God . . .*"

•

When he could speak, or think, he looked wildly around. As wildly as someone can look who is still fighting to swim up out of the murk.

He croaked, "Who shot? Who shot him? Where'd they go?"

"Shhh. Relax. Try not to talk for a minute, just rest. You're okay. I think."

"But who—?"

She patted her chest:

"You? No . . ."

She pressed her shirt against the back of his head to quell the bleeding. She freed up one hand and it dropped to her pants and she pulled up a very compact Walther semi-auto, 9-mil. Black.

"The James Bond gun," she said. "Always in my fishing vest. Remember, I go fishing by myself all the time."

"I . . ." He struggled to sit up. Made it to all fours. "We gotta go."

He'd been hit in the head before. By horses, in fights. It throbbed, it wasn't that bad. "We gotta go now," he said.

They heard a guttered moan and Jack straightened on his knees and they both turned. Cody was on his side gripping his left thigh where it gushed. He was in deep shade, ten feet into Ellery's. Then they heard the barks. Yips like shouts at first, then the snarls and building furor. Jack stood. Slight sway, steadied, it'd be okay. He grabbed her arm and tugged. "Gotta go now!"

He was already pulling her toward the cut strands and over them. Sounded like a hundred dogs, more bays now, then barks, and he could tell they were tearing down the hill.

"What about him?" she said, looking back at the guide on the ground.

"No time," Jack said. As he said it, Cody yelled, "Hey, fuck, hey! Just drag me across. They're electric-collared, they're collared!"

Jack gave her one more hard pull and looked back to see two packs of dogs pouring down through the trees. And then they were running upriver.

•

He had heard the frenzy before, the furious snarls and tearing. But before there had not been the smothered then gurgled cries.

•

Well trained or electric-collared, the dogs did not come after them. He could imagine them desperately charging back and forth along the invisible line between the posts, and then all along the intact fence. They ditched the rods. Just dropped them into the limbs of a box elder. And ran.

His head seeped but not badly. He felt nauseated, concussed for sure, but his gyroscope was intact, eyes clear. All he could hope for. He did not have a plan. There had been no Plan B, but as they hustled up the trail he remembered the phone on the desk in the main office. He expected the rip of automatic fire at any second, leaves shredding around them, but there was nothing. Because, he thought, as he pulled her along, whoever was watching could suddenly not see through the camera at the fence. Not an emergency, they had the dogs. But they sent Cody to keep an eye on them. To contain them if he had to. Maybe that gave them time. The mercs were probably up at Kreutzer's securing the kids, overseeing the treatments. Someone would have to call them. But there might not be anyone. Jensen might be in town or having lunch up above, or in his suite at the upper lodge, or wherever Jensen goes. If anyone heard any barking they might reasonably assume the dogs were running deer or a lion.

They did not take the steps up to the lodge but kept moving. Another quarter mile. Then they took the trail up to Jack's cabin. He shoved through the door, grabbed a tech shirt from the bureau, and threw it to her, took a bandanna off a hook and tied it around his head. He stripped his clumsy wading boots and waders and shoved on running shoes. She did the same, but had no other shoes. He yanked open a drawer and handed her two pairs of rolled wool socks. She'd have to wear her wading boots. Jack rebuckled the waist pack.

"Where are we going?" she said.

"The office. They have a phone. You've got yours, right? With Vince's number."

"Yes. And I know it by heart."

"Okay, good. We're gone."

They walked up to the office like two fishers looking to replenish flies and tippet at the shop. Like the strategy they'd just tried below wasn't working, maybe they'd buy a selection of foam hoppers or ants to use on top. Made themselves not run.

Guests paid enough to stay that the lodge might have let them take any flies they wanted anytime, but the pros know that even the richest people on earth love to pick out and buy flies. To comb over the open-topped display cases that are partitioned into hundreds of two-inch-square compartments, each with its tumble of simulated bugs, some so tiny they have to be handled with tweezers. Everyone loves it. The artifice of creating a mimic from tufts of feather and fur, and fine copper wire, to lace and spangle them with glittering Mylar thread, weight them with brass beads, and to size them from nearly microscopic to the heft of a hapless mouse—the flies contain the ingenuity and craft of fine jewelry and the promise of hours, days, in pursuit of something even more beautiful: a connection to the beating heart of the living earth and maybe to one's own mastery.

So if fisherfolk are not actually fishing, they love nothing more than spending hours at the shop refilling their fly boxes. If the shop gave the flies away it would degrade them, make the selection less critical, the foam box that held them in their rows less precious. The lodge knew this and so charged an outrageous $4.99 per fly. Tied by women in Thailand.

There was no one on the track as they walked up, no one in the parking lot, no one in the office as they pushed through the door. They heard a grinder winding in the big maintenance shed across the gravel parking lot, but that was it. Jack had covered the camera below so no one would know what had happened to Cody, and Jack doubted anyone had heard or noticed the shot, the yowls a mile downriver, down in the canyon and covered by the rush of numerous rapids. Once inside, he went straight for the phone behind the counter. Picked up the receiver, heard nothing, punched nine, the universal number for an outside line. Alison held up her phone with Vince's number on the contact screen. Jack waited. Nothing. Then a click, a woman's voice, "Can I help you?" She had an accent. Phew.

"Yes," Jack blurted. "Yes! Please connect with me with the following number—"

"I'm sorry, please give me your PIN."

"PIN?"

"Yes. This line is designated users only. Mr. Den, Mr. Jensen, and authorized PIN holders."

"I'm sorry," Jack said, trying to contain himself, "we have an emergency. A critical emergency."

"I'm sorry," the woman repeated, "we are not authorized or equipped to handle emergencies. But if you give me your PIN I can connect you."

Jack said, "Excuse me, people are dying here." He touched the back of his head where the blood had mostly stopped seeping through the bandanna.

"I'm sorry," the woman said. She sounded like she might be. But after all, people are dying everywhere.

"Well, can I call nine-one-one? That's all we need to do." He was trying to contain himself.

"You could, if you had the correct PIN."

"Where are you?" Jack said.

"Ireland."

Jack hung up. "Guns," he said.

"What?"

"I'm going for Den. The fucker's got a phone in his lair for sure. Then we're going to shoot our way out of here."

Alison laughed. Maybe it was nerves. Release. She had just pretty much killed a man. "Now you're talking like your uncle Lloyd," she said. And she said it as if she did not disapprove.

•

The gun safe was a closet. He knew it was not a true safe because Kelly had taken a key from a drawer when she'd stored his carbine. He slid out the desk drawer but there must have been a score of keys, all on color-coded tags and unlabeled. Unbelievable. The security at the lodge was a weird mix of paranoia and arrogance. The adjacent room that served as gift shop and fishing store had only one locked pine door in the far corner and he knew that his .30-.30 was behind it. The lock was a standard doorknob keyhole.

The counter in the fly shop had a wide desk drawer under the register. Jack rummaged away a roll of stamps, Super Glue, an ancient Corgi miniature Land Rover, and grabbed a tiny but long screwdriver, the kind used on laptops and glasses frames. "Gotcha," he said.

He zipped open the waist pack and dug around, pulled out the key to the gates at Tomichi Creek, which he still had. It was attached to the marlin bottle opener. He squatted and inserted the screwdriver and the marlin's spear of a bill into the keyhole and felt for the catch, pressed, and, using his knuckles, twisted the doorknob. Let out a breath and stood.

"Where the heck did you learn that?" she said.

"When I was coming up, Pop used to hide the Jim Beam in a closet."

"Right."

Well, at least they'd made a decent gun rack. The pegged slots held only four rifles: his .30-.30, two scoped hunting rifles, and an open-sighted AR-15. Perfect. He bet the lever-action Savage 99 was Cody's—kept here for easy access—the Winchester Model 70 had been Ken's, and the assault rifle Mr. Jensen's. Swiftly he let his hand run over the upper shelf and he found his two boxes of ammo and three thirty-round magazines for the assault rifle. There was also a magazine pouch hanging on a peg. "Thank you, Kurt, you motherfucker," he whispered.

"What?" she said.

"Nothing." He pulled out his lever-action carbine. "You know how to use this?"

She twisted her lips. "I shot my first white tail in eastern Tennessee when I was nine."

"Figured." He handed her the gun. "Here." And the two boxes of ammo. "Take this, too." He unhooked the Cordura shoulder pouch from its peg. "Put the ammo in this. Put this in there, too." He pulled one of the sticks of dynamite from his waist pack. "You've got your lighter?"

"Of course."

"This one's for me," he said, and he picked up the black AR-15. And Alison thought, *He's sure as shit's not bewildered anymore. He's frigging pissed. Me, too.*

CHAPTER FOURTEEN

They ran. Straight to the river. Avoided the parking lot by the front gate, the cart path that shot through the maintenance shed where they heard the grinder and someone working.

They crossed the main track that wound down past his cabin and entered the pine woods and made their way through them, then half slid down the bank through the trees to the river. They stayed in the lodgepoles and angled above the fisherman's bridge and the camera, working upstream. Before they got to Kreutzer's big meadow they swung away from the stream until they were at the edge of the trees and looking across the tall grass of the hayfield at the side of the big log building. Jack wanted to approach the front door from the side. He'd seen the camera over the entrance portico and it was aimed to cover the wide flagstone circle. He thought that if he stayed against the wall he could slip in from the side of the building and behind it. How he was going to get in the heavy locked front door he wasn't at all sure, but if he had to, a stick of dynamite would probably suffice.

They were crouched in the deep shadow with nothing but a hundred and fifty yards of hip-high hay grass ahead of them.

"Let me have your phone," he said.

She handed it to him and he stuck it in his pants pocket.

"Remember how to crawl?" Jack said.

"Some of my best years," she said.

They crawled. Elbow to knee. Stopped every twenty yards, breathed.

"Whew," he said.

"Toddlers are beasts."

"No shit."

When they were twenty yards from the side of the house he told her to move very slowly to their right so that she could see the front door. "The camera's covering the turnaround," he said. "If you stay back and at a wide angle from the entrance you'll be clear."

"Okay."

"If I come tearing out, shoot whoever's behind me."

"Okay." She tugged on his pant leg and he craned back. His face was grimed with sweat and blood and flecked with hay-seeds. She said, "What's the dynamite for?"

"Mayhem."

Her sudden smile tipped whatever fear into action. He racked the charging handle of the AR and tapped the bolt release. Like going over the horizon of a big rapid, he thought. You commit, paddle forward toward your line, and the trepidation falls away. Usually.

Here we go. He went. At a half crouch now to the propane tank twenty feet off the side of the lodge. Noted. Then to the log wall. He flattened himself and peered around the corner. There was the portico covering the front door. He could see the turnaround and the long drive through the grass. Checked his watch: 2:09. Respite. Should be. The stillest time of a summer day, when the downstream wind subsides and the upstream hasn't begun to blow. Like slack tide. Cicada time. He could hear the rising buzz of the insects in lazy waves. A movement caught his eye and he saw the golf cart bouncing up the drive. Perfect. Shay coming probably to fetch the lunch trays. She jounced to a stop at the entrance, nodding to whatever tune in her earbuds, probably rap, and bailed out. She went straight for the door. Pressed her thumb to the scanner and shoved it in. He knew she would kick down a doorstop and she did. He moved. Flat along the wall, under the porte cochere and through the door. But. She was there. Down a short hall in the great main room where two long pine tables held the wreckage of lunch. Her back was to him. She was shoving in a heavy chair, about to turn, probably to fetch a steel busing tray. On his right was a side table holding a hammered bronze vase filled with ferns and black-eyed Susans. Over it a muted oil painting of a man casting from a canoe on a misty lake. And just past the table was a door. Also heavy, not a closet. He lunged for it, cracked it enough to slip through, and shut it carefully and found himself at the top of a flight of stairs.

The smell hit him. Iodine.

Memories reside happily in smells the way swallows inhabit old barns. When Jack and his friend Wynn were on any kind of wilderness excursion of more than a day, and sometimes even then, they brought a first-aid kit in a one-quart stuff sack that consisted of ibuprofen, a bottle of iodine, ten Band-Aids of assorted sizes, and a few yards of silver duct tape wrapped around a broken half pencil. They figured that any wound they couldn't stanch with a piece of ripped T-shirt and a tight wrap of the tape . . . well, they were pretty much fucked. The iodine would disinfect it and ibuprofen would dull the edge of pain. And in a pinch they could use the iodine to purify water—five drops per quart—and the waterproof tape to patch a tear in a tent fly or down jacket. And they joked that if shit really got bad, they could sharpen the pencil with a clip knife and write a last will and testament. Never in his wildest dreams did Jack imagine that they might ever have to exercise that option. But they had used the iodine and the Band-Aids more than once to dress cuts, and he had always enjoyed inhaling the stringent sting of the tincture.

Now the smell hit him like the blast of a hospital ward. He blotted out the memory of Wynn and tumbled down the stairs as swiftly and quietly as he could.

At the bottom was a long hall lit with dim sconces and lined with doors like a hotel. Maybe where the resident workers slept—Shay, Cody, maybe Kurt, the mercs. The mercs. Where were the men in black? Taking a break, he guessed. By now, the afternoon treatment would be started. Guests and "donors" in their places, wherever that was. Everything humming smoothly. One or two of the men in black might be down below at the main lodge, just to be around in case he and Alison got feisty.

Humming smoothly. All the guests here for ten days, of mostly not-fishing. One or two "treatments" a day. Kurt said they're booked solid through October. The kids he saw were so clearly depleted. The dead girl, the boy very sick. How many rounds could they tolerate? How many guests? They would wring them out. So they had to have replacements. Somewhere nearby. And a constant supply. Of young people who had survived certain deadly diseases and had the right genes. And by the look of the children he had seen, they must have scouts in hospitals all over the world, Asia, Latin America, Europe. Jesus. And probably more than one of these centers. Den had luxury fishing lodges all over the world. Cody had mentioned a super-luxe lodge in Kamchatka. Last winter Jack had thought about guiding in New Zealand—it was their summer—and he had read a job ad, an essay, really, on a fishing website. It was "the most exclusive fishing lodge in Australia–New Zealand, at the head of Lake Wakatipu, offering ten-day excursions inclusive of half-days helicopter fishing, Michelin-starred farm-to-table food, and all spa services . . . seeking British or American fishing guides only." Jack thought it was odd. But foreign guides would be out of their element, dazzled by the luxury and the landscape, easier to manipulate and with no backup family nearby. Ten-day stays with half-days fishing . . . God. Who knows? Later—if there was a later—he'd check if that lodge was run by a company called Seven.

He needed to focus. He was here now. He stood at the head of the hall in the iodine reek and listened. Voices. Definitely. Muted but nearby. He took three steps forward and listened again. There. A clink, metal on metal. The first door on the right was not like the rest all the way down the hall. The others were standard size, stained pine, and had magnetic card locks as in a hotel. This one was wider, stouter, veneered in knotty cherry, with a wrought-iron lever handle. And a thumb lock pad.

WTF, he thought. He remembered the blond-bearded operator in black leading the line of kids, opening the front door, calling back to a "Taggart" to keep it down. Occam's razor, keep it simple. He leveled the AR-15 and knocked on the door. The voices ceased. All other sounds, too. Clearly an unexpected interruption, a rare hitch in protocol.

"Yes?" A hesitant voice, female. Wary.

Jack took a chance. "It's Taggart. The door lock scanners are down. I have a private message for William Barron."

Pause. He could feel his heart beginning a fast trot. Then he saw the door lever drop, the door crack. He shoved it in. The woman stumbled back. She was short, bespectacled, with short black hair going gray. In a white coat. Name tag Liu, mouth forming an O of surprise or outrage. And now he lifted his eyes and looked past her to two dozen faces lifted, turned.

A long room, softly lit. Thick carpet patterned like a tapestry, hinds in a wood. Pairs of what looked like dentist chairs upholstered in glove leather, each with a stainless box on a stand between them, clear tubes running from it to the person seated on either side. Adult, kid, alternating down the line, each to a pair. Red liquid in the tube running from the child, lemonade yellow from box to client. The machines all humming together. As Yumi Takagi had mentioned. But she had not mentioned the spaced floor lamps with amber mica shades stamped with Japanese maple leaves, or the piano concerto coming through hidden speakers. Or the spot reading lights extending from the backs of the clients' chairs only, which half the clients used to read magazines and books. He saw *Vogue* and *Outside* and *Yachting World*. The kids wore khakis, red polo shirts with the company trout logo. Jack saw the narrow door to what must be a changing room. Nor had the Takagis fully described the discreet Velcro straps, same color as the leather, binding arms to the arms of the chairs, legs to the half-raised ottomans of the recliners. Everybody raised their heads when Jack burst in, but the kids did so as if half-asleep, eyes swimming. Two doctors evidently—the woman Liu, holding to the back of a padded chair, and a tall man standing, white coat, dark hair, athletic—interrupted in the act of timing a client's pulse the old way, fingers on wrist, eyes to watch.

That image, of everyone turning to look. A freeze frame he could go over: Sir Will startled with something like outrage—what? . . . *him* . . . that gigolo guide? . . . what the hell? The Takagis, first chairs on the right, not shocked, but profoundly sad, and as if they had expected him. A couple he had not seen before, the man, gray-haired with bushy eyebrows, a face that seemed familiar . . . It was! The senator from New Hampshire when Jack went to school there. Jack thought he'd lost the election last fall, maybe this was his consolation. The Youngens, eyes wide but smiling weirdly.

In the suspended moment between the shock of surprise and the dread register of meaning, Jack pried Alison's phone from his jeans, swiped to camera, and held his finger to the shutter release and panned, then stuffed the phone home. Where was the boy? Halfway down on the right, eyes closed, asleep or unconscious. Jack moved. He would grab him. But the tall, supremely confident doc dropped his patient's wrist and called, "Who the hell are . . . You can't come in here! Hey!" And he stepped into the middle of the room to block Jack's path. Just on Jack's right, past the Takagis, was a well-coiffed woman in gold scallop earrings drinking tea from a heavy hand-glazed mug. The big handsome doctor stepped out to block him and Jack said, "Excuse me," and swiped up the mug and hit him so hard between the eyes he heard bone split and the blood spurted from the man's nose and he staggered back and crashed over the cowering woman doctor. Jack didn't wait. He turned to tear the tabs on the boy's straps, but stopped himself. The boy was clearly barely hanging on. If he carried him, especially into a firefight, he could kill him. Better to wait for help. He caught the eye of the girl who seemed to be his sister two chairs over and said, *"Ayuda. Yo voy. Salvando."* Her face was streaming tears and he thought she understood and he pivoted and flew out the door.

He needed to call for help and he was sure Den had the only working phone and he was sure, too, that he knew where Den would be. He ran up the stairs. Any second one of the doctors would press some alarm. Or call on some intercom he hadn't seen. At the top of the stairs he eased open the door into the foyer and looked through the crack, saw Shay stacking plates. Up, he was going up. He had been in a score of these fancy mountain houses. The first flight of stairs to the second story, he knew, would go up from the main room to a gallery. Right past Shay. He pushed through the door and ran. Past her. She whirled. Her shock.

"What the *fuck*?" she said. "You're crazy!"

He shook his head, put a finger to his lips, she blinked. Good enough. He saw the stairs. Floating fir treads ascending along one paneled wall. He bounded, two steps at a time. Yes, a gallery. It went around three sides of the great room; the fourth was the huge window facing meadow, the river, the canyon wall. Around the gallery he saw the expected doors to expected bedrooms. These were the super VIP suites, the super VIPs that had to remain super anonymous. What bullshit. All the doors had key card scanners except one. That would be it. Yes, bronze plaque, discreet, said, PRIVATE.

His thoughts were running fast, but skidded to a stop when he heard a booming voice yell, "You see the fucker? The new guide?" Jesus, he must have been in the basement, too. Or in the other wing. Where were the others. *"Shay!"* the man yelled. "Did you see him?"

Her voice cracked. "Yes!"

Jack froze. All he had to do was take three steps forward and look down over the gallery rail. He might get a good shot before the man returned fire, doubted it, the dude was a pro.

"Went out the front door!" she called.

Oh, damn, bless you, Shay. Wow. At some point you make a choice that defines the rest of your life. He tried the knob on the private door but of course it was locked. Nothing for it, the merc had run out the front. Jack kicked it in.

•

One steep flight. He knew that would be there, too. Up to the crow's nest. At the top no camera, good, but another cherry door and another thumb scanner. He didn't hesitate. He bounded down the way he had come. Got to the main room. Shay was standing over a table in a daze. He shook her. "Shay! Shay! Do you ever go up to Den's room? Above? Do you?"

She blinked as if waking. She nodded. "I bring him his meals sometimes. Or leave a shaker of martinis. God, you're a dead man."

"Can you get in? The scanner?"

Half nod. What he was asking now dawned, her nod turned into a shake of the head.

"Okay, come with me. Now!"

She stood, frozen.

"Now!" Jack said.

"I can't. He'll make sure my mother . . . He'll kill me."

Jack tugged the clip knife from his pocket, flicked it open. "Give me your hand!"

"*What?* What are you doing?"

"I'm cutting off your thumb."

She started to cry. Such a hard-boiled drifter, he never thought he'd see that. She nodded and led him back up the two flights of stairs. She put her thumb on the pad and Jack heard a *cheep* and he whispered, "Now get the hell out of here."

He raised the rifle to sight it and shouldered through the door.

•

And came face-to-face with a lion.

A huge male, roaring. Head raised, mouth open, all teeth bared. Mane as red as a strawberry roan's. What the h—? Simba! The full animal, stuffed and standing.

He saw no man. What he saw was a bank of tall windows circling the room and beneath them a band of video feeds. The screens were large and clear. Jack took in the monitors and recognized in succession: a dark mesh of what must be twigs at Ellery's fence; a steel gate he didn't recognize, must be Ellery's main; the riffle and long pool beneath the bridge, the rapid upstream; the riverbank above the KEEP OUT sign; the main lodge gate, both sides; Kreutzer's gate, both sides; Kreutzer's turnaround and parking area; aisle of dark trees and a flagstone path—must be from outside the kids' sleeping bunker; dimly lit room with twenty bunk beds: the inside; another doorway with stone path he didn't recognize; interior of a cabin—*his* cabin, POV he could tell was from the thermostat; main lodge bar; main lodge swimming pool.

He heard the scuff and then he saw it: behind the right ear of the lion the lifting stacked barrels of the over-under shotgun, big bore. It was just swinging up, behind the lion's head. Den had been crouching there. The shotgun swung up and Jack saw above it the tanned handsome face of the man, looking over wire-rim reading glasses, as if just caught working at a computer. Jack didn't think past that. The shotgun was swinging and Jack fired straight into the lion's mouth. Into the maw between Simba's open jaws.

He squeezed the trigger of the AR and fired off three fast rounds and saw a spray of sawdust out the back of the big head and flinched away hard at the concussive blast of the twelve-gauge, the one trigger pulled, and then Jack heard the window behind him to his left explode outward, and heard the screech of the man as he spun back and knocked over a monitor.

Jack flinched but sprang forward and saw the man flung face-down over a keyboard beneath the screens. An insulated cup leaking tea rolled off the edge of the desk and crashed to the floor. Smelled like Constant Comment. Next to the keyboard a phone. What he needed. The man leaked blood. One shot had hit apparently—not slowed too much by the back of a ten-year-old taxidermied skull—hit the man in the right chest. He screeched like some startled owl and sucked air which wheezed and chortled. Jack stepped in and with a hand and knee flipped the man onto his back. One lens of his glasses had cracked, the titanium frames bent.

"Den," Jack said.

The man gaped, both blue eyes open and blazing with scorn. "You're just . . . just a cowpoke." English accent.

"Yep, that's what I am. Don't fuck with a cowboy." Jack pulled out Alison's phone, swiped five times until he got to the naked girl being dragged across the barnyard. He shoved it in Den's face. "This is you," he said. "What are you doing to these kids?"

Den reached up with his left arm as if trying to grab the phone—to touch or claw, Jack couldn't tell. "She's just . . . no life," Den said. "Home . . . no life." He choked, coughed, licked dry lips, swallowed. "My clients run the world." Shot in the chest and still haughty. God.

"You shouldn't have said that. You're telling me that if you ever went to trial, you'd get off somehow—"

Den gaped to speak and Jack shot him twice in the chest.

He picked up the phone and then he cursed himself for killing Den too fast. Because the courteous operator said, "Good afternoon, Mr. Den. For security purposes, what is your PIN, please?"

•

He shook himself, rushed for the door. As he passed the lion he put one hand on the animal's rump in a kind of thanks.

Then the whole building shook and exploded.

It didn't explode but felt like it. At first he thought it was the propane tank. No ball of fire. Then he heard the stutter of an automatic weapon. Alison. The merc was shooting at her. She had waited, waited, heard the shots in the tower, seen the window blow out, and known: Jack was in the shit, way up in the attic, and needed a little help. And she'd lit a stick of the TNT and tossed it against the front of the lodge, probably the door. Now she was out in the grass somewhere in a firefight with a special operator.

Jack sprinted down the stairs, just let his feet windmill over the treads. He hit the great room, bottom of the stairs—caustic stench of scorched nitric acid, the smoke hanging in the room like a morning blasting fence post holes, but this wasn't fencing, it was killing. The bursts of fire were louder, just outside, and he edged to the corner and peered down the foyer. The front door was blasted off one hinge and leaned, and beyond it was a drift of lingering smoke. He ran to the maw and he could see Kurt's black pickup angled in the turnaround against the fountain statue as if it had skidded to a stop, and behind the engine block, shooting over the hood, was Blond Beard. He was shooting down the long drive, she was out in the meadow toward the front gate. No cover out there but grass stems. Where were the others? He heard another automatic rifle firing and the deeper boom of a larger caliber, probably Jensen with a handgun, probably a .45. Blond Beard was in profile and Jack could take him out. Don't rush it. Just like hunting. He raised the rifle and the man must have caught the movement. He wheeled and fired and Jack pulled the trigger and the man dove behind the truck where he was probably in view of Alison and Jack unzipped the waist pack and fingered out a stick of TNT and found the lighter beneath it and lit the fuse. He tossed it under the truck and ran out the front door, firing as he went.

The wheels of the truck lifted six inches off the ground in the blast and the gas tank blew in a second explosion and the whole vehicle burned.

He had remembered the red Tesla and prayed. It was parked to his left beside the front door. Beyond it was the black Jeep. Jack peered in the window and saw the key fob lying in the console. The new ones used voice commands; thank you, God, for old cars. He yanked open the door, threw the rifle in the passenger well, and jumped in; and, yes, the start button was big enough, obvious enough, and he thumbed it and the dash lit up like a pinball, and he pulled the automatic shifter to R and peeled a tight arc backward. He was aware that he was drawing more fire from the upstream corner of the building but everything had gone somehow silent, or muffled, as if the chaos and exploding shots were behind an unbreakable glass. The burning truck gave him some cover as he screeched down the driveway and made himself slow.

She jumped out of the grass like a jackrabbit, straight at the car, running low, and maybe three were firing now and she had the passenger door open and was in, didn't bother to roll down the window, just shattered it with the barrel of her gun so she could keep the rifle *and* close the door on the tiny cockpit, and before she had it latched Jack was moving.

He adjusted the rearview. Could see the turnaround in the mirror and the others moving. He saw three of them jump in the

Jeep, Jensen in the driver's seat and two others, and the Jeep swerved out of its parking spot and made a half donut and pointed down the drive.

Quarter mile. Long shallow S of a driveway. The torque of the electric car grabbed speed and shoved them back in the seats. The rusty steel wall of the gate loomed fast. Had to open it. He could see the keypad on its post. He jammed the brakes, skidded to a stop, cursed. The truck would be on them in seconds. He felt her hand squeezing his shoulder. Stay calm. "Take my gun!" he said. "Lay down fire right at the windshield. Point and shoot." She did. Kicked open the door, the truck screamed around the bend and she fired.

He punched in the numbers Kurt had given him. They were firing back, but on the move, bouncing over frost heaves. Nothing was hitting, not yet. And she was crouched behind her door and blasting in bursts of two. Her door wouldn't stop a bullet. The gate didn't budge. Of course not. Maybe he'd punched it wrong. He tried again, frantic. Nothing. Fuck fuck. Then their back window shattered and a hole tore into the dashboard. They were cooked.

"Got 'em!" she yelled.

And he remembered. Ana. Ana! She'd said, *Recuerde* . . . *Dígamelo* . . . Tell me so you remember. Her words on the porch. She'd insisted. *Tres, tres, nueve, tres.* Not a damn thing to lose.

He punched in the numbers and the big steel plates shuddered. And began to slide. Thank you, thank you. *Gracias a Dios y Ana—*

He glanced in the rearview, saw the Jeep's windshield had half shattered and spiderwebbed and the SUV caromed halfway into grass and stopped. Maybe she'd hit the driver. Maybe they were all dead. No such luck. The car backed out of the ditch and up onto the driveway and the front passenger was firing out his own window and the vehicle came on.

Goddamn, the gate was slow. But the Tesla was not that wide. Jack jammed the accelerator and they went through with maybe an inch to spare.

The g-force slammed them back into their seats and he was on the good paved county highway eating up the curves with the river and the tender greens of its cottonwoods flying by. The car hugged the road and the water smells poured in Alison's shattered window. With every mile he knew they were leaving the bastards in the dust. "Hey, here's the phone," he called over the rush of air. "All the photos." They gunned out into the open ranch country, alfalfa fields ahead and the bridge . . . "Tell him we're in deep shit and getting fired on and have the whole thing ready to send—"

"Got it." She was already typing fast with two thumbs, something Jack could never do. They took the turn at the bridge in a slide and whomped over the heavy planks and spun tires in the gravel on the other side. How many miles to phone reception? Maybe four, four more. All dirt for the next six miles till they intersected the highway along East River that led into Crested Butte. He'd have to slow way down. The roadster was heavy and did not do well on gravel; if they wanted to get there in one piece he'd have to slow. At least it wasn't raining. The sky was dark, boiling over the ridgetops, but the rain had held off.

They tore up through the groves of aspen, sliding in the switch-backs, slalomed around the scattered spruce, and topped the ridge and began to nose down. No one in his rearview. Good.

"Reception!" she yelled. "Got it! Sent!" Really good. And he let the elation rise in him like helium, and he looked out over the wider valley below and the paved highway and saw the bar lights flashing red and blue, two squad cars screaming down from Crested Butte.

Jensen had called them. Called in his compadres on a VHF or sat phone. Of course. Squeeze move. Jack could see that the SUV cruisers would get to the end of their road before the Tesla did. They would meet them head-on. The three heavily armed men would climb their tail. How many minutes behind? Two?

The crush in his chest was the knowledge. That he would lose again. What was he thinking? They were outnumbered, out-gunned, outplanned. Outmoneyed a million times. The deck was stacked and he would again lose someone he had grown to love. He had pulled her into this, and again, ultimately, he would be the killer.

Up ahead on the right was a gap in the trees and a rough ATV track descending into the ferns beneath the aspen. He smashed the brakes, skidded, and bounced onto the four-wheel-drive track.

•

They didn't make it far. Just far enough to drop into the slew of an old stock pond. Just out of sight of the road. Jack tried to stay on the highest edge of the track, but the tires dropped into the ruts and the frame scraped and the Tesla ground to a stop and they stepped out. They could hear sirens louder now, rising out of the valley. Then the gravel blast of a heavy vehicle on the road going too fast.

Without a word they reached in and picked up the rifles and slung them and they loped. Past the muddy pond it was more of a trail, and it contoured along the slope and they were trotting single file through the pale columns of the trees. Paler for the dark of the threatening sky. He thought they were like the columns of a church, or a catacomb. They slowed to a fast walk and kept on. Maybe two miles, three. They could no longer hear sirens, only the surges of the aspen leaves as the gusts swept through. There was nothing else to be done. The two pincers would meet and the Jeep would backtrack and they would find the trace, see the car. Then they would come after them, three trained soldiers at a run. Who even knew where Vincent Serra was. In St. Lucia? San Francisco? Who knew if he even had the vaunted connections she spoke of? A long shot.

Jack smelled water. They emerged into a narrow meadow and a view to mountains, close across a wooded basin. The meadow was flecked with asters and lupine. A tiny creek cut through it. They sat on rounded stones among the horsetail and listened to the burble. Neither had a word to say. They crouched and cupped their hands and rinsed their faces. The water was icy. Somewhere above them the last shaded patches of last winter's snow was melting.

And they could see them: the rags and tatters of snow on the sharp ridges of the peaks to the north. Not so far off. A half day's walk maybe. There would be ice blue gems of lakes up there, just above timberline, and just below it.

"Here," she said finally. "Let's take this off." And she reached for his bandanna and loosened it and carefully unstuck it from his hair and pulled it free. "Lemme see. Ouch. Let's rinse it."

He knew they should take cover, prepare for an assault. But he lowered himself to where his head was nearly in the dark water and she cupped her hands and washed the gash. He inhaled sharply. He was just sitting up when she put a hand on his arm. "Listen," she said. He froze. Then he felt for his gun in the horsetails.

"No," she whispered. "Listen."

He heard a stutter. Not firing this time but something on the edge of hearing, far off. She touched her ear. A roll, heard, then not, then steady, like a beating at the membrane of the afternoon, and then a drumming and he squinted under his palm and saw the two choppers coming over the divide. They came fast from the northeast, just over the sharp ridge of rock and snow and dropped down into the basin and the *thwopping* now was loud with a rhythmic pressure drop Jack felt in his chest. Two black Jet Ranger helicopters at speed, in formation. Close over the tops of the trees. They came straight across the drainage and as they approached their low ridge they banked south and went over.

A tear ran to the corner of her mouth. She blinked it back, tried, and her hand held to his arm. "Vincent," she said. "It's his people."

Jack could not yield. That this time he might not have to bear the loss. That there might be a reprieve. But. There was nowhere else those birds could be going; they were heading straight for the Taylor Canyon.

•

They stayed as the darkness thickened and true dusk filled the basin. It never rained and no one came. They lay down in the fescue on the far side of the creek and used the stiff horsetails for cover and watched the path until they could no longer see it. No one. Jensen and the operators must have seen the choppers, too, because they had Jack and Alison pretty much dead to rights, and did not come.

Kurt was generations in the valley and knew the country as well as anyone, and Jack was sure he had a self-extraction plan, and that's probably what was now occupying the three men.

Carefully they retraced their steps. It was a game trail more than anything and they lost it and refound it again and again in the dark. They held each other's hands for balance. The sky broke open and the moon floated in streaming clouds, lighting the night enough that they could finally see the aisles between the trees.

CHAPTER FIFTEEN

He went home. He helped Pop put up the last of the hay. In the afternoons, summer heat lay over the fields and the grasshoppers jumped ahead of the swather and by late afternoon the leaves of the cottonwoods gleamed the way they only do at the end of August and a fall cool settled into the valley. By nightfall the cold raised mist off the river. Sometimes in the evening he saddled Duke and they rode up onto the skirt of the Gore Range and looked north to the Never Summers and he could see the flush of gold spreading over the highest ridges as the aspen turned.

The home phone rang off the hook with calls from journalists and news producers and studio execs from around the world. They were trying to pump up the story and make him a hero and finally Pop unplugged the phone from the wall. In late September he was subpoenaed to appear before a grand jury in the US District Court for the District of Colorado and he drove down to Denver and gave testimony for two days. In the courtroom he felt like he was moving through molasses and he testified in a flat monotone and the judge told him more than once to take his time. He didn't see anyone else from the lodge.

At home, he and Pop didn't talk much. Sometimes at dinner they turned on the news and there was rarely a night without a Vampires of Taylor River story. Pop would say, "You sure?" and Jack would nod. "Kinda gotta see how it plays out." But he would stop his fork in midair and watch fascinated as if the newscasters were describing badly a dream that had meant much to him and that he could only partly process or recall.

The day the shit went down an enterprising young reporter for the local TV station in Crested Butte heard the frantic chatter on the police scanner and loaded the channel's one camera into her vintage Land Cruiser and raced up the Taylor Canyon. She followed two ambulances through the big gate and got there in time to see two Jet Ranger helicopters in Kreutzer's field and an FBI SWAT team ushering dazed guests out of the lodge and other agents and medics bringing the still drug-hazed kids from their bunker. In the footage they were again wearing the immodest hospital gowns, again walking as if windblown, and while Kayla Black was filming, two collapsed on the flagstones. Jack was told later that after Alison blew the door, and the fire-fight, and all the players with guns tore out of the compound, the team of golf cart drivers and employees at the main office had rushed up and herded the kids back to their bunker in the trees and told the guests to stay in their rooms until either a discreet extraction plan or a resumption of service was organized.

The footage was chaotic. There weren't enough ambulances, so the body of the operator next to the exploded truck was gurneyed to the back of a sheriff's department SUV and the big doctor who was out cold but whose vitals were strong was carried out to the back seat. They used the ambulances for the kids, four of whom were deemed critical. Kayla was fearless. She shoved the camera in the faces of the clients, who were so disoriented they forgot for critical seconds to cover them, and the media recognized at least half. She shrugged into an EMT's windbreaker that had been thrown over an ambulance mirror and dashed into the blown-open door of the house, holding the camera low and covered with her own jacket. And she had followed the commotion down the stairs and filmed chilling footage of the Vampire Pit and the Blood Chairs, as some outlets called them, with the clear tubes dangling and still half-filled with dark blood and urine-colored plasma and the recliners for the donors with the thick straps still hanging, looking like nothing so much as execution chairs.

After a few minutes, Pop would turn and study his son, whose forkful of food might be still halfway to his mouth. Only someone who knew Pop well could have read the pain, and if a tear ever ran from Pop's eye Jack didn't see it. Because Jack was transfixed, frozen. Sometimes—often—on the broadcast there would be snapshots of Jack and Alison: a photo of Jack from a canoe club trip in college, of him holding a paddle, smiling shyly, with a canoe beached on the bank of some river; Alison in full concert passion, gripping a mic and singing, and then always one of her holding a fly rod, taken with her father when she was a kid. Then mug shots of Kurt Jensen, Miles Bottini, and Adam Taggart, who were now on the FBI's Most Wanted list. And of the corrupt sheriff and deputy, who had driven back right into their own department's road block and been arrested. Pop would look at his son and say gently, "Enough?" and Jack would nod and Pop would pick up the remote and turn it off.

Once, as they ate in silence and looked west out the big window at a reef of dark rain squall blanketing the mountains and moving up the valley—the first rain of the fall and well needed—Pop said, "Jack? You did good. Remember that. You saved the lives of many people." The boy, anyway, Jack thought. They had rushed the unconscious kid to the clinic, from which he had been helivaced to St. Anthony's in Denver. He had survived.

"You saved people," his father said again. "You did."

Jack did not turn but put his hands flat on the table and looked down the valley at the veils of rain. They were curtains of night gray that curved against the wind and in them it was almost as if he could see the lives of his mother and of his best friend, their spirits, coming to him. It was not as if they lived, exactly, but maybe they were not lost forever to the great dark. That they endured in the weather and the seasons. The first gusts moved in the tops of the trees along the river and he cried. He let himself. It was the first time he had cried in the presence of his father since he was eleven and for the first time since then his father got up and came to him and held his shaking son.

She clambered along the boulders of the bank and stepped onto slab rock that sloped to the water and she waded to her knees and began to cast. The current was running low and clear. The Little Pigeon River ran out of the wooded ravines of the eastern Smokies, out of a wild country of cliffed gorges and dense rhododendron and mixed hardwoods of oak and ash and basswood, and thick forests of mute pines. This morning in early November the stream floated the leaves torn off in last night's squall. They were every color of fire—yellows, burnt reds, crimson—and the frost still lay in the shadows, and shreds of white mist clung to the ridges.

In a patch of sunlight a hatch of mayflies drifted off the water, and she casted up to the edge of a dark pool behind a slanting boulder and let the dry fly bobble down the seam. She wanted this. It was more than that, she needed it like food. Her rage-fueled song "Billionaire's Mile" had made it to the top of the charts in October, but it had brought her no peace.

Now she hummed. She had another song rising. It was half-formed, had not found its words yet, but it flowed out of an ache in her chest, out of images of cruelty and a pressure of hard loss, and of heartbreak, too. It was about letting go, which was in sympathy with the movements of the cast and the lengthening of the line. It needed to be sung and she would let it gather in her like a storm.

She had not seen any rises, but truthfully she didn't care if she caught fish. She just wanted to move against the fall current, smell the sweetness of turning leaves, and work the rhythm of the casts.

She was focused and she was singing. At first she did not hear the bird. The pitched call. And then it rose and carried with the wind upstream. She stopped humming and tipped her head and listened. It was a whistle. A Carolina wren. One of her favorites. The call came in threes and she let her fly fall to the water and she held herself very still. She listened. All the loss and grief rose up inside her, out of the places from which her own song had come. The wren cried. Alison turned in the river and the sun was on her face and she closed her eyes. *There is nothing better than this,* she whispered to herself. *You try. Try to believe it.*

When she opened her eyes she saw a fisherman at the bend. He was far away and backlit but she recognized the way he held the rod, the cadence of the casts. *Jack?* she thought. *My beautiful friend. It's Jack!* The wren's whistles were his. Three then three. He was fishing upstream. His line caught the sun with every cast. And the rhythm of it, and the way he moved with care and without haste, seemed as natural a part of the morning as a deer stepping to water.

Acknowledgments

Many people lent energy and insight to the making of this book. I am profoundly grateful to my first readers—Kim Yan, Lisa Jones, Helen Thorpe, Becky Arnold, and Jeff Streeter. And also to Jason Hicks, Bobby Reedy, Mike Reedy, Stephen Scaringe, Isaac Savitz, Willy Kistler, Karen Hammer, Jim Lefevre, and Landis Arnold for their invaluable expertise. Thanks to Adam Duerk, Lamar Simms, and Sascha Steinway for a better sense of the law. And to my doctor friends Melissa Brannon and Mitchell Gershten. Thanks to Donna Gershten for a certain voice. And to Maris Dyer for following through.

This book would not have been written without the guidance and encouragement of my extraordinary agent, David Halpern, and my brilliant editor, Jenny Jackson. You were both with me from the first pages, and to you both I raise a glass.

To everyone above: I am humbled by your generosity, wit, and wisdom. It is an honor and a privilege to know you all.

TWO FRIENDS.
THE ADVENTURE OF A LIFETIME.
A WILD RIDE.

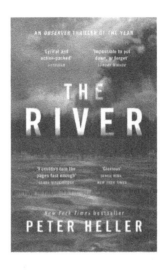

A GRIPPING TALE OF MAN VS NATURE, AND THE DESTRUCTIVE POWER OF REVENGE

One of the *Observer* thrillers of the year:
'Glorious prose and razor-sharp tension'

'I couldn't turn the pages fast enough'
Clare Mackintosh

'Glorious drama and lyrical flair'
Denise Mina, *New York Times*

PROLOGUE

They had been smelling smoke for two days.

At first they thought it was another campfire and that surprised them because they had not heard the engine of a plane and they had been traveling the string of long lakes for days and had not seen sign of another person or even the distant movement of another canoe. The only tracks in the mud of the portages were wolf and moose, otter, bear.

The winds were west and north and they were moving north so if it was another party they were ahead of them. It perplexed them because they were smelling smoke not only in early morning and at night, but would catch themselves at odd hours lifting their noses like coyotes, nostrils flaring.

And then one evening they pulled up on a wooded island and they made camp and fried a meal of lake trout on a driftwood fire and watched the sun sink into the spruce on the far shore. Late August, a clear night becoming cold. There was no aurora borealis, just the dense sparks of the stars blown from their own ancient fire. They climbed the hill. They did not need a headlamp as they were used to moving in the dark. Sometimes if they were feeling strong they paddled half the night. They loved how the darkness amplified the sounds—the gulp of the dipping paddles, the knock of the wood shaft against the gunwale. The long desolate cry of a loon. The loons especially. How they hollowed out the night with longing.

Tonight there was no loon and almost no wind and they went up through tamarack and hemlock and a few large birch trees whose pale bark fluoresced. At the top of the knoll they followed a game trail to a ledge of broken rock as if they weren't the first who had sought the view. And they saw it. They looked northwest. At first they thought it was the sun, but it was far too late for any lingering sunset and there were no cities in that direction for a thousand miles. In the farthest distance, over the trees, was an orange glow. It lay on the horizon like the light from banked embers and it fluttered barely so they wondered if it was their eyes and they knew it was a fire.

A forest fire, who knew how far off or how big, but bigger than any they could imagine. It seemed to spread over two quadrants and they didn't say a word but the silence of it and the way it seemed to breathe scared them to the bone. The prevailing wind would push the blaze right to them. At the pace they were going they were at least two weeks from the Cree village of Wapahk and Hudson Bay. When the most northerly lake spilled into the river they would pick up speed but there was no way to shorten the miles.

~

On the morning after seeing the fire they did spot another camp. It was on the northeastern verge of a wooded island and they swung out to it and were surprised that no one was breaking down the large wall tent. No one was going anywhere. There was an old white-painted square-stern woodstrip canoe on the gravel with a trolling motor clamped to the transom and two men in folding lawn chairs, legs sprawled straight. Jack and Wynn beached and hailed them and the men lifted their arms. They had a plastic fifth of Ancient Age bourbon on the stones between the chairs. The heavier one wore a flannel shirt and square steel-rimmed tinted glasses, the skinny one a Texans cap. Two spinning rods and a Winchester Model 70 bolt-action rifle leaned against a pine.

Jack said, "You-all see the fire?"

The skinny one said, "You-all see any pussy?" The men burst out laughing. They were drunk. Jack felt disgust, but being drunk on a summer morning didn't deserve a death sentence.

Jack said, "There's a fire. Big-ass fire to the northwest. What you've been smelling the last few days."

Wynn said, "You guys have a satellite phone?"

That set them off again. When they were finished laughing, the heavy one said, "You two need to chillax. Whyn't you pull up a chair." There were no extra chairs. He lifted the bourbon by the neck between two fingers and rocked it toward them. Jack held up a hand and the man shrugged and brought the fifth up, watching its progress intently as though he was operating a crane. He drank. The lake was a narrow reach and if the fire overran the western shore this island would not keep the men safe.

"How've you been making the portages?" Jack said. He meant the carries between the lakes. There were five lakes, stringing south to north. Some of the lakes were linked by channels of navigable river, others by muddy trails that necessitated unloading everything and carrying. The last lake flowed into the river. It was a big river that meandered generally north a hundred and fifty miles to the Cree village and the bay. Jack was not impressed with the men's fitness level.

"We got the wheely thing," the skinny man said. He made a sweeping gesture at the camp.

"We got just about everything," the fat man said.

"Except pussy." The two let out another gust of laughter.

Jack said, "The fire's upwind. There. We figure maybe thirty miles off. It's a killer."

The fat man brought them into focus. His face turned serious. "We got it covered," he said. "Do you? It's all copacetic here. Whyn't you have a drink?" He gestured at Wynn. "You, the big one—what's your name?"

"Wynn."

"He's the mean one, huh?" The fat man cocked his head at Jack. "What's his name? Go Home? Win or Go Home. Ha!"

Wynn didn't know what to say. Jack looked at them. He said, "Well, you might get to high ground and take a look thataway one evening." He pointed across the lake. He didn't think either of them would climb a hill or a tree. He waved, wished them luck without conviction, and he and Wynn got in their canoe and left.